Dugout Jinx

The Chip Hilton Sports Series

For more information on
Chip Hilton-related activities and to correspond
with other Chip fans, check the Internet at
www.chiphilton.com

Chip Hilton Sports Series
#8

Dugout Jinx

Coach Clair Bee
Updated by Randall and Cynthia Bee Farley
Foreword by Dean Smith

BROADMAN & HOLMAN PUBLISHERS

Nashville, Tennessee

0-8054-1990-X

Published by Broadman & Holman Publishers,
Nashville, Tennessee
Page Design: Anderson Thomas Design, Nashville, Tennessee
Typesetting: PerfecType, Nashville, Tennessee

Subject Heading: BASEBALL—FICTION / YOUTH
Library of Congress Card Catalog Number: 98-28093

Library of Congress Cataloging-in-Publication Data
Bee, Clair.
     Dugout jinx / by Clair Bee ; [edited by Cynthia Bee Farley,
Randall K. Farley].
          p.   cm. — (Chip Hilton sports series ; v. [8])
     Updated ed. of a work published in 1952.
     Summary: After graduating from high school, Chip is
invited to join the Parkville Bears as a summer intern, and
he manages to save the Bears' season—and his own baseball
future—from being spoiled by the schemes of an
unscrupulous man.
     ISBN 0-8054-1990-X
     [1. Baseball—Fiction. 2. Conduct of life—Fiction.]
I. Farley, Cynthia Bee, 1952–   . II. Farley, Randall K.,
1952–   . III. Title. IV. Series: Bee, Clair. Chip Hilton sports
series ; v. 8.

PZ7.B38196Du   1999
[Fic]—dc21   98-43531
                                                          CIP
                                                           AC

              2   3   4   5   6   04   03   02   01   00

TO

HAROLD UPLINGER

Student, Athlete, Friend

CLAIR BEE
1952

TO

MICHAEL CLAIR FARLEY

Our son and Clair Bee's grandson

Only in reflection do we discover
where He has led us
and where and how
He has prepared us for each step of
each journey.

You have enriched our life with such joy,
and we are proud of you.

LOVE,
MOM AND DAD
1999

Contents

CONTENTS

Foreword

WHEN I WAS ten or eleven years old, as World War II started, I was forced to read books by my parents. Since I liked athletes, I read and enjoyed several books by John Tunis that dealt primarily with baseball, as well as sportsmanship. Now fast forward to the summer of 1959, when at long last I had the opportunity to meet acclaimed basketball coach Clair Bee.

Frank McGuire was a close friend of Coach Bee, and I had just finished my first year as an assistant to Coach McGuire at North Carolina. Coach Bee was helping Frank with his basketball books, *Offensive Basketball* and *Defensive Basketball*. They had asked me to select two topics for chapters in *Defensive Basketball,* so we spent a great deal of time together that summer at the New York Military Academy.

During this period, not only did I stare at the painting of the fictional folk hero—Chip Hilton—that was on the wall behind Coach Bee's dining room table, but I had the opportunity to read some of the Chip Hilton series. The books were extremely interesting and well written, using sports as a vehicle to build character. No one did that better than Clair Bee (although John R. Tunis came close). By that time, Bee's Chip Hilton books had become a classic series for youngsters. While Coach Bee was well known as one of the great coaches of all time, due to his strategy and competitiveness, I believe he thought he could help society and young people most by writing this series. In his eyes, it was his "calling" in the years following his college and professional coaching career.

Coach McGuire and I, along with countless other basketball coaches, learned basketball from Clair Bee. The point zone, which Coach Bob Spear and I developed at the Air Force Academy, had its origins in one of Coach Bee's old books on the 1-3-1 rotating zone defense. We made our point zone at Air Force to be more of a match-up zone, but this is just one instance where people on the basketball court today still depend on innovations by Clair Bee.

From 1959 until his death, I visited with Coach Bee frequently at the New York Military Academy and at Kutsher's Sports Academy, which he directed. He certainly touched my life as a special friend. Not only does he still rank at the top of his profession as a basketball coach, but he now regains the peak as a writer of sports fiction. I am delighted the Chip Hilton sports series has been redone to make it more appropriate for athletics today, without losing the deeper meaning of defining character. I encourage everyone to give these books as gifts to other young athletes so that Coach Bee's brilliant method of making sports come to life and of building character will continue.

DEAN E. SMITH
Head Coach (Retired), Men's Basketball,
University of North Carolina at Chapel Hill

CHAPTER 1

What Price Glory

PARKVILLE BASEBALL fans were pretty much like other fans all over the country. If anything, they were possibly more loyal to their hometown team—first, last, and all the time; win, lose, or draw. In addition, they believed their aggressive Eddie Duer—balding, eagle-beaked leader of the Parkville Bears—was the craftiest manager in the game, miles ahead of his contemporary diamond impresarios. Duer's latest brainstorm was creating such excitement in the fanatical baseball city of Parkville that Bears Stadium was jammed with fans that Tuesday morning, even though the Bears weren't practicing and weren't scheduled to play until the following Thursday night.

Parkville's fans had flocked to the stadium to get a good look at the year's high school stars from eight different states who'd been selected to compete in Duer's inaugural and highly touted festival of baseball talent: The World's Greatest Amateur All-Star Tournament.

DUGOUT JINX

Most of the 120 young athletes had already registered for college and were looking forward to four more years of study and baseball. However, some were on a last vacation before going to work. Whatever their plans, every player in the tournament was eager to gain recognition as a prospect for major league baseball—especially with the first-year player draft just days away. Each player was also determined to prove his team was the best in the tournament.

There were a number of unfamiliar faces in Bears Stadium that morning too. They included neatly dressed men who were obviously devoted to baseball. Many of them wore shirts embossed with their team logos, and a few fans noticed their championship rings as the men positioned radar guns to check pitching speeds. The fans sitting near the men sized them up, noting their analytical eyes, tanned faces, and well-conditioned physiques. A few spectators understood why these professionals were so far from the close division battles and the down-the-stretch dogfight, wild-card races taking place in the American and National Leagues for final play-off spots. These sun-browned strangers were baseball experts, prospectors looking for new talent!

Most major-league organizations and the Major League Scouting Bureau were represented in the group of keen-eyed scouts watching the agile teenagers working out on the sun-baked diamond. There were a few freelancers in the stands, too—men who scouted or "bird-dogged" for new baseball talent on their own. These independents were paid for every player they recommended to an organization who made the grade in the minors, and they later received a bonus if the player made good and went up to the big leagues.

The team working out that Tuesday morning was only one of eight teams the scouts were there to watch.

The baseball experts would be able to see more than one hundred top notch baseball prospects from eight different states in three short days. Who knows; maybe the next Sammy Sosa, Alex Rodriguez, Cal Ripken Jr., or Roger Clemens was out on that field wearing a high school uniform. Not the finished product, of course, not one of the grand old masters—the Sultan of Swat, Joltin' Joe, Stan the Man, or Rapid Robert, but a true diamond in the rough. For scouts and fans alike, this was baseball heaven!

Stu Gardner, veteran scout for the Drakes, was one of the few scouts watching who already knew most of the players on the field. Gardner had spent several weeks watching and waiting for two of the players batting and throwing down below to graduate from high school. His eyes shifted from the tall, blond teenager leisurely warming up in front of the third-base dugout to the bulky first baseman taking part in the infield practice. The fan sitting on his right interrupted his thoughts.

"I figure you're a scout," the man ventured. "Is that right?"

Gardner smiled. "That's right," he said, without taking his eyes off the scene below.

"Who do you like out there?" the fan asked.

"That's easy," Gardner said quietly. "I like the two kids from Valley Falls, the pitcher warming up in front of the dugout and the big left-handed first baseman."

"You ever see them before?" the man on Gardner's left queried.

Gardner smiled ruefully and nodded his head. "I sure did," he said. "I watched those two kids for two months while they were in high school, just waiting for them to graduate, so I could talk to them about our organization and our plans for them in the upcoming draft."

"What did graduating from high school have to do with it?"

"Well," Gardner explained patiently, "our club plays the game according to the rules. According to the rules and according to ethics," he added. "You see, my boss, the general manager of the Drakes, knows a high school athlete isn't eligible for the draft until he's earned his high school diploma. As far as that's concerned, he never feels too bad when a youngster says he wants to wait until after he's graduated from college. So we watch the kid's progress and maintain contact with him all the way through college, until he earns his degree. Then when he becomes eligible for the draft, we hope to make him a top pick. But we better not lose him then!"

"What'll happen to those two players out there now that they've graduated from high school?"

"As far as my club is concerned, nothing. They want to go to college. Once they enter college as full-time students, they most likely will not be eligible again for selection until finishing their junior year. Anyway, a player who signs a contract automatically becomes a professional, and that eliminates him from college ball in that sport."

"Couldn't you sign them anyway? I mean, can't somebody sign and go to college and keep his mouth shut and play college ball just the same?"

"Well, I guess he can if he's that kind of person," Gardner said slowly, "and if the person who signs him has that kind of character."

"I say a kid ought to get all he can get while he can get it!" someone behind Gardner asserted loudly.

Gardner turned his head to face the speaker. "Some kids just aren't like that," he said softly. "Kids have dreams and ambitions. Sure, the money's important, but it's secondary to their love of baseball. See that pitcher warming up? He could have gotten—can still get as far as that's concerned—a hefty bonus just to sign with the team that drafts him, but he's going to college."

"He must be crazy!" the fan in the back said loudly.

"Or rich!" someone added.

"No," Gardner continued, "he's not wealthy by a long shot, far from it. In fact, he worked all through high school, and his heart is set on following in his dad's footsteps by getting his degree and playing college ball."

"I still think he's crazy," the fan behind Gardner insisted.

"I know plenty of kids who'd jump at the chance he's passing up!"

"What price glory!" someone said dryly.

"Money isn't everything, you know," Gardner said quietly. "Baseball's my business, and I'd give my right arm to have my club draft and sign that kid out there to a contract. But if he were my son, I'd be awfully proud of the stand he's taken. Some kids aren't for sale and can't be bought. They value their dreams and ambitions far more than money. He's that kind of kid."

"You know any of those other kids out there? Any other Plainsmen?"

Gardner shifted his eyes from position to position before answering. "Yes," he said, nodding his head, "I know most of them. That is, those who seem to be better prepared for a beginning career in professional baseball. I scouted the state high school tournament when these kids were chosen to represent the Plainsmen. The player catching Hilton is from Valley Falls too. His name is Soapy Smith. He's a fair catcher but not in a class with Hilton or Cohen. Cohen's the first baseman."

"You sure seem high on the pitcher. What did you say his name was?"

"Chip Hilton. He's the best big-league prospect I've seen in a long time, and I've seen a lot of them."

"He must be something!"

Gardner smiled grimly. "You'll see," he said confidently, "if you're here tomorrow night when the Plainsmen play the Rebels."

"Look, mister," the fan said proudly, "I'll be here *every* game. We're baseball fanatics around here! Every ticket for the series sold out three days after they went on sale. Eddie Duer's a good manager, and he knows how much this place loves baseball too."

Someone added, "We're afraid one of the big-league teams will offer him a chance to manage up there, and we'll lose him."

"How about some of those other kids out there? Any of them as good as that Hilton? I mean, in their own positions."

Gardner shook his head, scanning the field reflectively. "No," he said firmly, "none of them are in Hilton's class. The first baseman is about the next best." He gestured toward the field. "That's a great collection of kids, though, and I could be wrong about some of them, especially the outfielders. The Plainsmen will be playing in the final game Saturday afternoon, or I don't know baseball. Well, I'm off to get a hot dog and a Coke. See you later. Enjoy the games."

Gardner wasn't necessarily hungry, but he wanted to get away from the quizzing. He liked the friendly fans, but he had work to do. As he walked up the concrete steps toward the food court, he remembered his first meeting with Chip Hilton and Henry Rockwell, the high school coach. As Stu reached the last row of seats, he paused and looked down on the field, thinking about the tall, blond pitcher.

Stu Gardner knew Chip Hilton all right. Stu guessed he knew him almost as well as if the young hurler had been his own son. He'd watched him fight back after an ordeal that would've gotten the best of anyone's courage. He'd seen Chip outsmart three local cheats who'd tried to use him in their grandiose scheme to get rid of Coach Rockwell.

For the next ten minutes Gardner relived those three hectic days he'd spent at State University when Chip had pitched his team to a great opening-round victory only to become the victim of a last-minute plot. The plot was diabolical, and it partly succeeded. It would have succeeded entirely if Chip hadn't been a fighter, a winner who didn't know when he was beaten.

Chip Hilton had been framed by a cheap criminal who had used an innocent autograph on a bogus baseball contract to keep the star hurler from pitching the championship game. The state high school athletic committee had declared Hilton ineligible the morning of the final game, and the fiendish plan would have succeeded if Chip himself had not exposed the plot a few hours later.

Stu Gardner was in on the finish—in on it at the very moment when, only by chance, Chip had recognized the one person in the world who could have been the instigator of the fraud. Stu smiled as he remembered the car chase and how he'd been in on the fight and the capture of one of the hoods. Then he'd seen Chip pitch the last nine innings of a nineteen-inning game, only to lose the pitchers' duel when a teammate misjudged an easy fly, and a foul ball hit a pebble and rolled into fair territory scoring the runner. It had been a tough loss for the youngster, but Chip Hilton had taken it like a champion.

"And that's what he is," Gardner murmured aloud, "a real champ!"

Gardner, deep in thought, was startled to hear a familiar, irritating voice. He heard the voice again. It didn't take long to pinpoint the speaker who was gesturing wildly and talking loudly to a group of fans who seemed to be getting a big kick out of the conversation.

"Oh, no," Stu Gardner sighed. "Here's trouble!"

He studied the man's shrewd, pasty face. "Gabby Breen," he muttered. "He *would* show up!"

Nelson "Gabby" Breen was a shrewd, hustling, fast-talking fast dealer with absolutely no scruples. The tall, stoop-shouldered man was dressed in flashy clothes, and his breezy, nonchalant manner, his loud voice, and his garrulity attracted attention everywhere—and he enjoyed it. Given a few minutes in any group, he could advertise himself so well that every person within the sound of his voice soon knew he was a baseball scout and a self-proclaimed sports agent.

Early in the spring Breen had agreed to scout for the Hedgetown Raptors and had rapidly wormed himself into the confidence of Steve "Boots" Rines, their manager. He had also positioned himself to attract the attention of the owner of the Hedgetown club, Hunter Kearns, and had used his talents to ingratiate himself into the good graces of that worried baseball mogul.

The Raptors, Hedgetown's pride, had won the minor league division pennant the previous year. In the off-season, Boots Rines had been successful in recommending that team management make only a few changes in their championship roster for the current year. However, the Parkville Bears had strengthened their team, gaining several of the same youngsters Gabby Breen had urged Rines to recommend to Kearns.

More importantly, the Parkville Bears had taken the league lead early in the season and held it all the way. It was now easy to understand why the relationship between Kearns and Rines was strained. Breen hadn't helped the situation, despite his apparent friendship with Rines. The wily scout had his sights on the manager's job and was working insidiously toward that objective.

"You Bears have got yourselves a pretty fair bush league club," Breen continued loudly, "but you'll never win the pennant!"

"Why not?" someone challenged. "We're out in front and just have to stay ahead of the Raptors."

"Raptors will take all ten of those games," Breen retorted, "easy!"

"Not with Scissors pitching," a fan yelled. "You just watch him cut the Raptors down again Thursday night!"

"Aw, Scissors Kildane's just a boy scout," Breen said disdainfully. "All he has is a glove and a prayer!"

"He shut out your has-been team the last time out!"

Breen's face flushed, but his burst of anger passed quickly. When he spoke, there was no trace of antagonism in his voice. "Rines *gave* you that game and used his weakest pitcher on the hill."

"I suppose Lefty Turner's a weakling!" heckled another Bears fan.

Breen laughed boisterously. "Turner? He was giving the Bears a break."

Changing the subject, he gestured toward the high school all-stars on the field. "Don't tell me you Parkville fans are fallin' for this little-boy stuff? Has Duer got everyone in this place hyped up over these high school kids? What's this all about?"

"*You* know what it's all about," someone chided good-naturedly. "You know, or you wouldn't be here. Guess Rines is getting worried. Must have sent you over here to do a little spying on the Bears or else you're scouting for new talent!"

Breen laughed. But this time it was a strained, forced laugh. "Boots ain't interested in this all-star game stuff. He's just focusin' on winnin' the pennant. But I'm different. I thrive on findin' young players and developin' them into big-league prospects. In my territory over the last few years, I've signed about thirty kids, and 'bout half of them are big-show stuff, baby!"

"Any in this league?"

"Sure, lots of them! You got one of them playin' right here in Parkville. The best keystone operator in the business!"

"You mean Corky Squill?"

"No one else! I had the Bears organization draft him before I agreed to work for the Raptors."

"He's good all right," a fan acknowledged grudgingly, "if you go for that kind of ballplayer."

The man behind Breen tapped him on the shoulder. "If you're looking for a solid first baseman, you don't have to look any further than that kid out there right now," he declared. "Watch him!"

"Strange as it may seem," Breen said loudly, "that's exactly what I'm lookin' for." He gestured toward first base, "That big southpaw the one you mean?"

"Watch him throw."

Breen grunted. "Huh, the kid's got an arm, all right, but he's gotta be a hitter too."

"He can hit! See the red roof of that house over the right-field fence? Well, he bounced two or three monster shots off the roof a little while ago during batting practice."

"Means nothin'," Breen said lightly, with an exaggerated gesture. "Let's see if he does it in the game where it counts."

WHAT PRICE GLORY

Sitting several rows behind and to the left of this odd assortment of baseball enthusiasts, Stu Gardner was seething. He suspected Gabby Breen was a phony who cared nothing about young players, except to exploit them for his own benefit.

Gardner had heard rumors about the ways Breen used to impress young hopeful players. The man had exploited every athlete who had been unfortunate enough to believe the wily schemer's promises of glory in the major leagues. Breen was trouble for young kids with big-league ambitions. Trouble with a capital *T.* What sort of intrigue was he cooking up now in that devious mind?

CHAPTER 2

A Taste of the Future

WILLIAM "CHIP" HILTON would have been greatly embarrassed if he had known anyone in the ballpark was talking about his baseball prowess with so many other outstanding players thronging Parkville for the tournament.

Right now, Chip felt so right, so perfectly relaxed, that he wasn't thinking about anything except his pitching. He was basking in that zestful feeling that comes to a hurler who is "on." Chip's fastball was hopping and his slider was twisting a mile. Still he didn't throw himself away. He knew when he'd worked his arm enough, and he was pacing himself and willingly called it a day when Pat Reynolds, coach of the Plainsmen, called, "That's it, team! Hit the showers!"

Chip put on his warm-up jacket and was just heading for the dugout when Reynolds called him, "Come here a second, Chip. I want you to meet someone you should know."

Chip glanced at the young stranger who had joined Reynolds. He was tall, almost skinny, and his height dwarfed Chip's six-foot-two. Chip figured he was a good six-six and in his early twenties. "Must be a basketball player," he speculated to himself. "He's sure tall enough." His interest quickened.

"Chip," Reynolds said proudly, "I want you to meet Alex Kildane. I guess you've of heard him."

Chip nodded eagerly and extended his hand. He'd heard of "Scissors" Kildane, all right! Who hadn't? Kildane was the rookie sensation of the Midwestern League, already tabbed for the majors and regarded as the greatest pitching find since Nolan Ryan.

Kildane's long fingers twined around Chip's hand like steel bands as the slender hurler pumped Chip's arm and smiled down at him with friendly, gray-green eyes.

"Hi, Chip," Scissors greeted him warmly. "I've heard about you too! Pat's been talking about you all morning. Says you're the best pitcher in this tournament."

Chip reddened and shifted his weight. He was flustered with himself for being embarrassed. He tried to say something, anything coherent, but the words wouldn't come.

Reynolds saved him. "Scissors wants you to appear on his local TV show tonight, Chip, and I told him you'd be tickled to death."

Chip wasn't tickled to death, but he wasn't able to say anything. He just nodded his head and smiled until suddenly the words came.

"I-I don't think I'd be any good, Mr. Kildane."

"Call me Scissors," Kildane said lightly. "And you'll be all right, leave that to me. I'll pick you up at your hotel at 7:15. OK?"

"OK," Chip agreed lamely. "OK, I guess."

Later that afternoon as he sat in the bleachers watching another team go through their practice, Chip regretted being so agreeable and wished he didn't feel so self-conscious so often. When eating dinner that evening with Biggie and Soapy, he was so unusually quiet that his longtime friends became suspicious and eventually pried the news from him.

"With Scissors Kildane!" Soapy blurted. "Oh, man, I'm up for that! Let's go!"

Much to his surprise, Kildane had three passengers in his car a few minutes later when he pulled away from the Park Hotel and headed for the studio. The three boys had never been on a TV program and were bewildered by the confusion of the cluttered scene when they arrived on the set. Scissors Kildane, however, seemed right at home, and Chip wished he could feel as comfortable as the easy-mannered, confident pitching star.

"Guys, have a seat over here," Scissors directed. "They've got to get me beautiful for the camera. Won't be a second."

There were four sets in the room, and Chip's eyes filled with amazement. The *Scissors on Sports* set was lit, and cameras were positioned as crew members ran through last-second details, waiting for Kildane to return from makeup. Another set in a corner of the big room displayed a modern kitchen. A third set was being readied for the *Parkville Today* talk show, and the last set featured a home improvement show.

"Man," Soapy, eyes wide, whispered. "It's like watching four channels at once. I could get used to this!"

In a few minutes Scissors was back, walking with a teenager about Chip's age. "Chip," he said, "I want you to meet Jon Gordon. Jon, this is Chip Hilton. You two should get acquainted. You're pitching against each other tomorrow night."

Jon Gordon was about Chip's height and almost the same weight. The two pitchers shook hands and smiled, and then Chip introduced his two friends. "This is Soapy Smith, Jon. He's our catcher," Chip explained. "Biggie plays first base."

Gordon shook hands with Soapy and Biggie, and they stood there, awkwardly shifting from one foot to the other. Kildane broke the silence. "Chip, from what I hear, the Plainsmen and the Rebels are pretty evenly matched. It ought to be a good game. How do you think you'll make out?"

Soapy startled everyone by snorting loudly. "We'll kill 'em," he said aggressively. "Kill 'em!"

There was a shocked silence until Biggie rolled his hamlike hand into a big fist and then shook it menacingly at the exuberant Soapy. Soapy's pretense of innocence and Chip's laugh eased the situation.

"Now you're seeing the real Soapy Smith, Jon," Chip said lightly. "He's at his best when he's trying to get into the act."

But Soapy didn't take Chip's remark at all lightly.

"Do you think I could, Mr. Kildane?" the redhead blurted, as his eyes shot in Scissors's direction. "Do you think I could get into the act—get on the show? Man, if I ever went back home and told them I was on your show—"

Scissors had no chance to answer Soapy's question. The director gave Kildane the cue, and before Chip knew it, he was standing beside Jon Gordon in the background of the set, and Scissors Kildane was talking away as easily as if he were in his living room.

"Good evening Bears fans. The much publicized high school All-Star baseball tournament has been the vision of our manager, Eddie Duer. The Drakes, our parent organization, and all of us Bears think it's one of the best things he's ever done to strengthen the organization and promote baseball here in Parkville. It's no secret Eddie's hoping our organization drafts some of these young players. From the talent I've seen out on the field, I hope we get some of them, especially a couple of the pitchers.

"And that brings me to some eligibility and first-year player draft information I'd like to read to you: 'Major League Baseball Rules establish player eligibility for the upcoming draft, the First-Year Player Draft. A player is eligible to be drafted if he's a resident of the United States or Canada and hasn't signed a major- or minor-league contract. High school players are eligible for the draft if they've graduated from high school and haven't attended college. College players must have completed their junior or senior years or be at least twenty-one years old. Junior college players, regardless of how many years they've completed, and twenty-one-year-old players are eligible for the draft.'

"You know, every All-Star on these eight tournament teams has been warmly received in town, and I'm sure they appreciate all that Parkville hospitality. And now, baseball fans, I want to introduce my special guests."

While Kildane had been talking, Chip's thoughts had wandered. Maybe he'd be a Scissors Kildane someday. . . . Maybe he had made the wrong choice about going to college. . . . Kildane wasn't more than three or four years older, and here he was making a lot of money playing baseball, had his own show, and was in a position to do things for his family. . . . Maybe Chip Hilton ought to forget about college and an education and think more about his mom. . . .

Chip looked up, then, and nearly burst out laughing. Soapy had his thumbs in his ears and was wiggling his fingers and making faces at Kildane. But the freckle-face feigned innocence when Kildane caught him. Scissors laughed, too, but he managed to go on.

"Fans, on my right is Jon Gordon, a southpaw who will start for the Rebel All-Stars tomorrow night. On my left is Chip Hilton who will pitch for the Plainsmen. In just a moment I'll come back to these two star hurlers and ask them some questions about their pitching and get acquainted.

"But first, I want to remind you that at nine o'clock tomorrow morning, the Rockies meet the Lakers in the opening game of the tournament. Immediately following that game, the Miners and Mountaineers tangle, and, in the late afternoon, the Yankees and the Buckeyes square off. Now, let's get to our guests, the players who will start the nightcap game.

"Jon, have you ever pitched night ball before?"

Gordon seemed right at home. "No, Mr. Kildane," he said calmly. "I've never pitched a night game, but I'm excited about it."

Kildane turned to Chip. "And how about you, Chip. Have you ever pitched a night game?"

Chip was surprised at his own voice. He was talking, all right, but the words seemed to come from far off and sounded like those of a stranger. "Yes, Mr. Kildane, I've pitched at night, but never in a big-league ballpark. It's got me a little worried."

"That's nothing," Scissors laughed. "I get worried too. Every time I look for the catcher's signs and see those big clubs waving around, I get plenty worried. But, you know, pitchers have the edge in night games. It's the hitters who really have to worry. There are lots of shadows, the background is poor, and if a hurler has a lot of fast stuff—or breaking stuff—he's got a big edge on the hitter.

You know, hitters don't wait 'em out much at night. I figure that's particularly true of high school players, and that's why control is so important.

"Another thing, if your fastball is working, use it early and then fall back on your breaking stuff later.

"You're going to get a lot of fun out of this series, and you're going to like that mound out there and this Parkville crowd. You've never played baseball before a crowd like this one. So, Jon, what's your pitching forte?"

"I'm supposed to have a little bit of speed and control, but I don't have much soft stuff. In fact, my coach said he doesn't think I'll ever correctly learn the change up."

Kildane turned to Chip. "Chip, suppose you tell our viewers just what you expect to throw against Jon and his team tomorrow night."

Chip shook his head and smiled. "I'll try to use my fastball, just as you said, at the start. Then work a little bit on my slider, and . . . well . . . I guess I'm like Jon. My coach, Henry Rockwell from Valley Falls, used to tell me my sweeping curve was my change-up pitch."

Kildane laughed. "That's me all over," he said. "I throw a hard one and then I throw an easy one, and that's my change of pace. Well, now, aside from pitching—"

"Excuse me, Mr. Kildane," Chip interrupted. "I'd like to see how you hold your knuckler. I've heard Mr. Reynolds talk about it, and I'm working on a blooper pitch—that's what I call it—but I don't know whether I'm holding it right or not."

Kildane nodded his head approvingly. "Sure, Chip. Someone toss me a ball. I'll show you how I hold my knuckler. Keep in mind that you can grip the ball against your fingertips, fingernails, or knuckles. I hold mine with the thumb and two outside fingers and then dig my first two fingernails on the seams. The important thing is to use the same sort of windup and throwing motion. That's where the deception is. You see, it isn't the pitch as much as it is the deception of the windup.

"Now you and the viewers can see how I'm holding the ball, but in a game I try to conceal it as long as possible. All pitchers try to do that, try to keep the ball hidden from the batter as long as possible and then use the same motion in the windup as they do for their fastball.

"Now, that's enough about pitching. Let's talk a little bit about hitting. I heard Pat Reynolds say you're a switch-hitter, Chip. Which side do you like best?"

"Well," Chip said awkwardly, "I'm not a very good hitter, but I like to bat from the first-base side of the plate best because I'm that much closer to first, and when I follow through on a hit, it pulls me around in stride and helps me to beat out infield hits."

"From what Pat tells me, you don't hit many on the ground," Kildane chided. "He says you hit a long ball—and often! How about you, Jon? How do you hit?"

"I hit from the third-base side of the plate. It may seem funny since I'm a southpaw, but I never did learn to hit from the other side. In fact, when I do get over on that side, I can't seem to focus on the ball."

Kildane nodded knowingly. "There might be a reason for that, Jon. I'm glad you brought it up. Everyone has a dominant eye, usually the right eye for lefty hitters and the left eye for righty hitters. Switch-hitters, like Chip, can focus either eye according to the side they're hitting from. Viewers, I want you to try something. Now do just as I say. First, close your right eye, put your hand over it, and focus your left eye on the ball. Got that? Now cover your left eye and focus your right eye on the ball. What happened? The ball moved when you changed from right to left and left to right, didn't it? All right, try it again. Chip, you and Jon try it too."

Just as Kildane said, the ball seemed to change positions. When Chip closed his left eye, the ball jumped to the left and up, and when he closed his right eye, the ball jumped to the right and down. He'd never thought of that before. Maybe he could work with this knowledge and improve his hitting.

"That's fine," Kildane concluded. "Now, Chip, here's a bat. Stand just the way you do when you're at the plate. Let's see your stance and how you hold the bat when you're batting from the third-base side of the plate. That's it! Hold it! Now swing right through just as if you were batting. Take a full swing."

Chip swung the bat through in a full arc, finishing with the bat back over his left shoulder.

"Now, let's try that on the other side from the first-base side of the plate. Watch closely, folks. He's a fine hitter from either side of the plate, and he seems to have the same form from both sides. Now, Chip, pull the bat through just as you did before. Try to imagine you see the ball coming and you're going to knock it out of the park, just like you hope to do tomorrow night."

Chip pulled the bat through in a clean level sweep and ended with the bat over his right shoulder. He felt foolish posing that way, but Kildane ended his embarrassment when he slapped him on the back and took the bat away.

"There you are! Now you know why Chip Hilton is a good hitter. Me? I can't hit the water when I jump out of a boat.

"We don't have much time left, but I've got a couple of other All-Stars I want you to meet. This is Soapy Smith from Valley Falls. Soapy plays with the Plainsmen in the tournament and is a catcher. In fact, he caught Chip

Hilton in high school. Soapy, just what does this battery mate of yours throw? He's been a little modest, hasn't he?"

"He always is," Soapy chirped. "You know, Mr. Kildane, I never saw you work, but I'll bet you haven't got half the stuff Chip's got!"

Kildane chuckled. "You don't have to tell me that, but you can tell our audience."

"Hi, sewers—" Soapy began and then stopped. His eyes were fixed and wide, like a deer's frozen by the headlights of an oncoming car. Soapy was stagestruck. His hand flew to cover his mouth, and he looked painfully at Kildane.

"Soapy, do you mean *viewers?*" Kildane offered.

"Uh . . . right! Hi, viewers. Chip's got a lightning fastball, and he's got a screwball, and he's got a blooper and a good change-up curve, and he's got a slider and some kind of underhand twister that even I can't catch. He fools the batters and me too!" Soapy finished with a rush. He had rehearsed what he was going to say, but the camera light had mesmerized him and almost tongue-tied the loquacious clown.

"That repertory would fool most anybody," Kildane said dryly. He turned to Biggie Cohen. "Fans, Biggie Cohen is another All-Star from Valley Falls. He's about six-four, weighs two-thirty, and plays a mean game at first base. You played football, too, didn't you, Biggie?"

Biggie nodded his head. "Yes, Mr. Kildane. I played four years at tackle."

"Pat Reynolds tells me you're a southpaw and an ideal first baseman. A pretty good target for your infielders, I'd say. How do you hit? From the left or the right side of the plate?"

"I'm a southpaw hitter. I hit from the first-base side of the plate. I don't know much about that dominant eye stuff you've been talking about, but I can't hit a thing from the third-base side of the plate."

"You do pretty well from the first-base side though.

"Well, everyone, that just about cleans the bases until tomorrow night when I'll have some more All-Stars for you to meet. So, until then, this is Scissors Kildane saying, 'So long.' Good luck to Jon Gordon, Chip Hilton, Soapy Smith, and Biggie Cohen. See you at the stadium!"

Kildane shook hands with each player and said, "Nice job! You guys were great! Give me a couple of minutes to get this junk off my face, and I'll take you back to the Park Hotel."

Half an hour later, Scissors Kildane dropped everyone off at the hotel and thanked them again. In the lobby, they ran into Pat Reynolds and Stu Gardner, the Drake scout, who slapped Chip on the back.

"Mr. Gardner! It's great to see you! I didn't know you were here!"

"Oh, yes, I've been around," Gardner said quietly. "By the way, we watched the show. You guys were a big hit!"

"I ought to hit someone," Biggie grumbled, glaring at Soapy.

"Did you really like it?" Soapy asked innocently.

Gardner nodded. "We sure did! Particularly the part where Chip and Jon were talking about the game tomorrow night. By the way, Chip," Gardner warned, "Jon's tough! He's got an awful lot of fast stuff. You'd better be ready for tomorrow night. Anyway, let's get together tomorrow or the next day, Chip. I've got a lot of things to tell you."

"I'm ready to call it a day," Biggie suggested. "We've got to be rested for tomorrow night, or we're goin' home on the midnight express."

A TASTE OF THE FUTURE

Chip, however, couldn't get to sleep that night. The brief glimpse of professional baseball, the television interview, the exciting life Kildane lived, and the atmosphere of good fellowship flooded him with dreams of his own future. College seemed far away at the moment. Then he thought of his mom and her deep desire for him to get a college education. He also thought about Biggie and Soapy and his friends at home. For a long time they had planned on going to State together and "taking over," as Soapy would say. Then there was "The Rock." Henry "Rock" Rockwell, his old high school coach, was now moving to State to join the coaching staff in football, basketball, and baseball.

Chip had never taken part in a college football practice, but he had received an invitation to State's freshman football practice. Chip's four friends had been invited too—Biggie, Soapy, Speed Morris, and Red Schwartz. Chip's thoughts shifted to football and the thrill of competing against other players for a place on the starting team. There would be more than one hundred athletes, all trying out for the team.

College was going to be a lot different from high school. When a guy went to college he was supposed to grow up, assume responsibilities, get ready for the future . . .

CHAPTER 3

One-Act Play

SCOUTING AND PLAYER development is crucial to the success of any major-league organization. It was no wonder, then, that twenty or more baseball experts had staked out Parkville to evaluate the talent at the eight-state high school All-Star tournament orchestrated by Eddie Duer.

Searching for and developing big-league players is a serious business. Scouts have the enormous responsibility of laying the foundation for their team's future success. Every big-league chain has fifteen to twenty-five full-time scouts in its player development division and lots of "bird dogs," or part-time scouts.

Each big-league organization invests many millions of dollars each year to put the best possible team on the field for their fans. In addition to the cost of fielding a major-league team, their farm-team budgets must support scouting expenses, minor-league player bonuses and salaries, and the instructional and training camps conducted for young hopefuls.

ONE-ACT PLAY

Scouts are a friendly and loquacious bunch. When they get together, a thousand stories of players discovered and signed are told and retold. In the early days of organized baseball, great discoveries were easy to sign. That's no longer true. Since every major-league team has its own scouts and also utilizes the Major League Scouting Bureau, outstanding players are generally known to practically every organization, so the discovery of a gold nugget is rare.

Today, the big challenge is to be sure all homework is done before draft day. On "d-day" each year, the first-year player draft is conducted by a conference call among all the major-league clubs. Taking turns, teams select players in reverse order of their won-loss records based on the previous regular season. National and American League teams alternate selections, concluding after a maximum of fifty rounds.

It doesn't end there. Even after a player has been selected, the challenge remains to sign him to a contract with the club. If the player enters a college, the team loses its rights to sign him, and a draft selection is wasted. The player may simply choose not to sign with that team, hoping to be selected by another team in a future year's draft. That's where building a relationship becomes important. Often it means talking to the athlete's family, his close friends, his minister, his high school coach, and even a lawyer or agent to get the player's signature on a contract.

After the players had dinner and had gone to their rooms, the scouts, sportswriters, and fans remaining in the lobby and coffee shop of the Park Hotel began talking about the visiting All-Stars and the close race between the Bears and the Raptors. Stu Gardner was talking to some of his friends, and each time Gabby Breen tried to maneuver closer to Plainsmen manager Pat Reynolds, Stu discreetly positioned himself to block Breen's every move, much to Reynolds's amusement. Pat had heard a lot about Gabby Breen, and he was determined to cooperate with Gardner to protect Chip Hilton and Biggie Cohen from the tricky scout.

Later that evening Reynolds surprised Gardner by asking him to sit in the Plainsmen dugout during the tournament.

"Is that allowed?" Gardner asked.

"Sure, just as long as you don't talk business to any of the kids. I guess we don't have to worry about that."

"You can say that again," Gardner agreed. "I'm only interested in Hilton and Cohen, and they made it very clear—and so did Henry Rockwell—that they'll be full-time students at State in the fall. But when those two kids finish college, my club will be there come draft day."

Despite Chip's almost sleepless night, he was up early and pulled a protesting Soapy and a grumpy Biggie out of bed. After herding them downstairs to the hotel's restaurant for breakfast, they walked the few blocks to the stadium to watch the Lakers-Rockies game. The Lakers were far too strong for the Rockies and won easily, 12-7. After lunch, the three boys were back in the stands when the Mountaineers and the Miners tangled. The game was tense and tight, a pitchers' duel all the way, with the Miners winning 1-0.

The Yankees-Buckeyes game was close and interesting; but in the top of the seventh, when the crowd stood up for the stretch, Chip, Biggie, Soapy, and the rest of the Plainsmen started for the locker room to get ready for their own game with the Rebels. After the entire team was dressed, Pat Reynolds took time to run through the Rebels' strengths and weaknesses and then let the team watch the last inning of the Yankees' 6-3 win over the Buckeyes.

Dusk was falling when the Plainsmen took turns in the batting cage for hitting practice, and the lights flashed on at 7:30, flooding the field as spectators began streaming into the stands. Bears Stadium was a first-class ballpark with a well-constructed red brick grandstand with newly decorated spectator sections stretching from first and third bases nearly to the bullpens in the left- and right-hand corners. Chip walked out beside the mound and tossed two or three balls to the hitters to get the feel of the mound and the lights.

Suddenly, Reynolds yelled out. "Chip, get out of there! You're liable to get hit! Warm up in front of the dugout."

While Chip was warming up, Reynolds sat beside Gardner in the dugout. "I think we can win the whole thing, Stu," Pat said confidently, "if I can get two good games out of Hilton."

"You'll get two good games from Chip, all right, Pat," Gardner declared. "He's the best young pitcher I've seen in a very long time. If he's on, you won't have any trouble with any of these teams. What are your plans?"

"I plan to work Chip tonight, go with Rick Parcels in the next one, and then come back with Hilton on Saturday. That'll give Chip three good days' rest, so he ought to be OK. I'll use our other two pitchers as relievers since none of these high school kids are used to nine-inning games."

Chip, wearing his warm-up jacket, sat down at the corner of the dugout bench. Reynolds dropped down beside him and put his arm across Chip's shoulders.

"Chip," he said, "this is your big game. I know you've played some night games, and I heard Kildane give you those tips last night. Everything he said was right. Use your fastball early. Get ahead of the hitters whenever you can and stay with the hard ones. Then you can use your breaking pitches and soft stuff. Beyond that, I want you to pitch your own game. How do you feel?"

"I feel good, Coach. I'm loose and my arm feels great."

"Good! We've got a good hitting team, Chip, and I don't think you'll have to bear down all the way, but you'd better stay ahead during the first few innings. Another thing, you've got a good fielding team behind you, so don't try to do it all yourself. Right?"

"Right, Coach," Chip said firmly. "Would it be all right for Soapy to work with me?"

"Of course, Chip. If you want Soapy, well, Soapy it is! I'll work him for five innings and end up with Overton. Get together with the two of them and go over your signs. We don't want any slipups. Good luck, Chip. Give 'em all you've got."

Up in the stands, Gabby Breen was back in the middle of the same crowd from the previous day, and it seemed almost as though yesterday's conversation had never ended.

"There's your big lefty out there on first," someone said.

Breen watched Biggie as the Plainsmen whipped the ball around the bases. As he watched, his shrewd eyes narrowed. His concentration did not pass unnoticed.

"Well?" someone asked.

Breen was cautious. "Not bad," he said amicably, "but even I can play catch."

Just at that instant Biggie took one of Rico White's throws from deep short. The ball was far to Biggie's right, but the big left-hander shifted his feet with lightning speed, extended himself in a full stretch, and made a successful glove-hand stab. Then, gathering his feet under himself skillfully, he pivoted rapidly and fired the ball to Soapy Smith straddling home plate. It was a big-league move, and Breen knew it. So did the fans surrounding the flashy stranger.

"You can do that, too, eh?" the same voice persisted.

"No-o-o," Breen drawled. "But let's have a look at his batting."

Breen glanced into the Plainsmen's dugout, and his keen eyes narrowed angrily as he studied Stu Gardner sitting at the end of the long bench. "No ethics," he muttered to himself, "absolutely no ethics." A few moments later the game was on, and Breen made himself concentrate on the play and on the slender blond pitcher who toed the rubber for the Plainsmen.

Seconds later Breen forgot about Stu Gardner, the friendly fans around him, and everything else as he watched the kid on the mound rear back, kick a long leg toward third base, uncoil, and throw a blur of light down the alley with effortless ease. Before Chip had thrown a dozen pitches, Breen was elbowing the man next to him.

"What's that kid's name? The pitcher out there?"

"His name is Chip Hilton. Has a great reputation in his home state."

When the Plainsmen trotted in for their time at bat and the Rebels took the field, Breen was sitting on the edge of the seat. His eyes were glued on the tall, graceful athlete with the wide, sloping, power-packed shoulders who was making his way toward the Plainsmen's dugout.

"Three up and three down," Breen muttered, "and they ain't even seen it yet!"

DUGOUT JINX

Gabby Breen hardly looked at the Plainsmen's hitters and didn't even know when they managed to push a run around so Chip would have something to work with. Breen was watching Chip and Gardner as a cat watches a mouse, and he was puzzled. When Gardner neither looked at nor spoke to the pitcher, he was even more puzzled.

"What's the deal?" he muttered. "Gardner's no fool. How come he's in the dugout? That old fox ain't sittin' in that dugout just to keep away from the crowd."

Breen continued to worry as Chip kept mowing down the Rebel hitters. As the innings passed, with Chip steadily crafting a no-hitter, Breen's pasty complexion took on a pink hue, and his heart thumped faster and faster. Gabby had known lots of young pitchers who could go for five, or six, or even seven innings, but this kid got stronger as he went along! When a third strike got away from Soapy Smith and the hitter went all the way to third on Soapy's bad throw to second, Breen noted that the kid on the mound stayed cool, calm, and collected.

Suddenly it was the bottom of the ninth, and the big kid was still blazing the ball past the hitters as if he were in a hurry to get home. With the last pitch, Gabby Breen was on his feet, cheering the young hurler as the Plainsmen hugged and high-fived their All-Star pitcher to celebrate Chip Hilton's chalking up a no-hitter!

Breen glanced at the row of goose eggs stretching clear across the scoreboard in the Rebel frames, but he never noticed the five runs and the nine hits the Plainsmen had collected. For the first time in a ball game, Gabby Breen didn't even know the score. As he hurried toward the exit, his thoughts focused on an important call he had to make. In his excitement, he didn't even realize he'd completely forgotten about Biggie Cohen, the star first baseman.

Breen had difficulty reaching his contact as he huddled in the telephone booth next to the convenience store. Gabby was very cautious about protecting his various business deals—especially this kind of deal. He was careful to avoid leaving traces and left nothing to chance. That was the reason for the call from the phone booth, instead of using his cell phone or the phone in his hotel room.

As he waited, Breen drummed his fingers on the metal coin box. This had been a good day. He now knew there were two possible big-league players in Parkville, and he meant to make them his. He had concentrated on Biggie Cohen first, simply because he had a deal lined up to produce a good first baseman. But he'd almost jumped out of his flashy shirt when he'd watched Chip's smooth delivery as the big, broad-shouldered youngster poured his fastball down the alley. The boy's effortless speed reminded him of Roger "Rocket" Clemens's first years in the big leagues.

Finally, long past midnight, his thoughts were disrupted by the completion of his call. Before he realized it, he was shouting. "Look, the kid's got it! Throws a fireball. Throws it easy too! He's more 'n fast! You know he's throwin' a baseball, 'cause you can see it when the other kids just chuck it around, but when he drops that long arm behind the back of his leg and spins and kicks his left toe—brother, you don't see no more baseball! It must look like a marble comin' to the plate! Why, the kid catchin' can't even hold him. . . . Tonight's the first time I saw him and I gotta move fast! Gardner's here and he's not here for the fresh air. I gotta have some money. . . . Yeah! Now! . . . When? . . . Can't you make it sooner? . . . All right! But hurry! This deal's hot and it's gotta be big and fast! Gardner's close to him but I don't think his club is interested. Besides, Gardner's a boy scout, too honest for his own good. That's why I know he . . . That's what I'm tryin' to tell you. Gardner wouldn't break his word if it cost him his life, and that's why I know he hasn't approached the kid about the draft. He'll probably head for the kid's hometown right after the game Saturday afternoon anyway. . . . Valley Falls. I know where it is, but I'm gonna close on the kid and sell him before he gets home. Look, I can twist him around my finger. Leave it to me! He won't get out of my sight. Can you get the money here? . . . OK. S'long!"

Getting up early was nothing new to Chip Hilton. He was used to opening the Sugar Bowl in Valley Falls before he went to school. So it wasn't strange that he woke up early the following morning and promptly pulled the covers off his protesting roomies, laughing at their sleepy, yawn-punctuated pleas for "just ten more minutes."

"Why are you gettin' up in the middle of the night," Soapy grumbled, tugging the warm covers back over his head. "Where are you goin' anyway? What's the rush? We don't play till this afternoon!"

"Yeah, and Coach Reynolds said to sleep late," Biggie added. "Of course, you don't have to work today, so you can take it easy."

"What's the plan for this mornin' anyway?" Soapy demanded.

"Chalk talk in the team room at ten," Chip explained, "lunch at eleven, and on the field at one o'clock. Come on. We'll jog, then come back for breakfast."

"Jog!" Soapy yelled. "Who wants to get out of this nice warm bed to jog? Not me, man!"

Chip persisted, and Soapy finally gave in since he knew it was the only way he'd get breakfast. They were a few minutes early for Coach Reynolds's ten o'clock meeting. Their Plainsmen teammates were reading the story of the game in the morning papers. But they weren't too busy to greet their three friends from Valley Falls.

"Hi ya, Chip! You see the papers?"

"Look! They got your picture plastered all over the sports page!"

"Nice hitting, Biggie. Here. Read the story!"

"What's the paper say about me?" Soapy demanded. "What's the matter with those scribblers? Don't they ever give catchers any real credit?"

Pat Reynolds arrived at that moment, ending Soapy's comical tirade. The next hour was devoted to studying the notes Coach Reynolds had prepared on the Yankees hitters and the team's fielding weaknesses.

Like Chip, Gabby Breen didn't sleep late that morning either. He had lots to do, and he wasn't going to waste any time. He spent most of the morning in the archives of the Parkville *Gazette* checking the sports pages from the Valley Falls *Times* and *Post*. He wanted to know more about William "Chip" Hilton, and he was amazed by what he discovered. He couldn't understand why major-league scouts hadn't been camping on the Hilton front lawn. *How could a kid like this be overlooked? Something's not right here! What am I missing?* Breen wondered.

The thought disturbed Breen, and he passed a restless morning, scanning paper after paper and reading about Chip Hilton. When the Plainsmen took the field that afternoon, Breen was in his usual seat, watching Chip loosen up and observing every move Cohen made on first base. The longer Gabby thought about the two players, the more impatient he became. He wished the special delivery service would hurry up with that check.

"Decide on anyone?" one of the fans asked curiously.

"No, not yet," Breen admitted slowly, "but I've got my sights on two or three of them." He eyed his questioner. "You know, we got sort of a gentleman's agreement not to approach any of these kids until they get back home and the draft has taken place."

"The big first baseman one of them?" a fan persisted.

"Yes and no," Breen fenced, "but I can tell you one thing: I can spot a good prospect quick as anyone. Some guys gotta follow a kid around all year. Not me!"

"How about the kid who pitched the no-hitter yesterday? Bet you got your eye on him," someone declared.

Breen smiled mysteriously. "Could be," he said. "He could be one of them, and then it could be someone else."

"Well," someone said cynically, "you'll have a tough time winning over some of the players in this tournament. A lot of big names are hanging around. You've got lots of competition for the draft."

Breen laughed loudly. "Yeah? Let me tell you something, my friend. I can get any player I want! Look, I've been in this game a long time. Here's the way I win."

Breen leaned closer to the surrounding heads and lowered his voice. "When I'm after a kid, I figure out what it takes before I make a move. Sometimes I work it one way, and sometimes I work it another.

"One of my special strategies is what I call the clincher. I make an appointment with a kid at his home, in the evening, so a parent will be around. Then I turn up carrying my briefcase. After I've talked to them and gotten them interested, I suddenly lean down, spring open the briefcase, and dump a mountain of cash right out on the floor! Right on the floor! That gets 'em! Then I sit back and say, 'Sign this contract and this is just the beginning.' I shove my contract under their noses and before you can say 'World Series ring,' I got the kid signed, sealed, and delivered." Gabby crowed, "Clever, eh?"

Breen's listeners nodded and gazed at him with new regard in their eyes. They believed Gabby's boast as if it were real inside stuff.

Gabby leaned back, satisfied with his performance. He noted the awe in the naive faces of his listeners, and he almost chuckled aloud. These baseball rubes didn't know it, but he'd been rehearsing his one-act play for a kid by the name of Chip Hilton.

CHAPTER 4

Number One!

SOAPY SMITH, muttering to himself, was standing in the center of the players' tunnel leading to the field, and he was itching to get out there. He spat in his glove, thumped the pocket with the closed fist of his right hand, and gestured toward center field. "Well," he stated smugly, "now we know who we have to beat for the big trophy on Saturday afternoon!"

"Knock it off," Biggie growled. "You wanna jinx us?"

Chip glanced at the scoreboard. It was the last of the ninth, no one on, two down, two strikes on the batter, and the Miners were leading the Lakers, 4-3—and that's the way the game ended. The Miners would be one of the tournament finalists.

Minutes later the Yankees took batting practice. The Plainsmen then took their licks and fielding practice. Finally, Reynolds called for a huddle in front of the dugout.

"All right, kids," Reynolds began briskly. "This is it! Parcels—you start! Overton—you work behind the plate!

NUMBER ONE!

Here's the batting order: White, Degnan, Mariani, Cohen, Chambers, Erickson, Roberts, Overton—and Ruiz, you're the designated hitter for Parcels. Williams, you're the first sub. Let's go!"

Reynolds ordered Soapy, Chip, Sheffer, and Lennox out to the bullpen with instructions for Soapy to have Sheffer and Lennox ready.

"Chip, throw just enough to loosen up. You won't be doing any pitching today, but I may use you as a pinch hitter."

Chip had never been in a regular bullpen in his life. It was a strange feeling to watch his teammates from the left-field corner. He seemed too far away to help much, and Chip especially wanted to cheer Rick Parcels. He would always remember the righthander's sportsmanship in the championship game when Valley Falls and Salem had fought a nineteen-inning battle for the state championship crown. Salem had won that game and Chip had lost the pitchers' duel to Rick when a batted ball lit foul, spun into fair territory, and enabled the runner on third to score the winning run. But Rick Parcels's gracious sportsmanship had eased the sting of that defeat.

After a few throws, Chip sat down on the bench facing the infield to watch the game. Soapy, Bill Sheffer, and Bob Lennox joined him, and the four teammates sat watching Rick Parcels's masterful pitching. Rick was great and never in trouble. When the Plainsmen came in for their turn at bat in the bottom of the sixth, leading 5-0, Reynolds sent Rick Williams out to tell Soapy to get Bob Lennox warmed up and come in with him to catch the rest of the game.

"Yes-s-s!" Soapy celebrated. "C'mon, Bob! Let's go!"

Then, with every pitch, Soapy began to chant: "Chip, Rick, Bob, or Bill—if one doesn't do it, the other will!"

Soapy was still rapping when he and Bob Lennox started for the diamond, and Ken Overton trudged out to the bullpen.

"Nice going, Ken," Chip said. "Rick must have been great."

"He was that!" Overton agreed. "Coach sent him to the showers."

The Yankees sent Bob Lennox "to the showers," too, in the top of the ninth. They began one of those inexplicable hitting sprees, scoring two runs and filling the bases with none down before Coach Reynolds called time and waved for Bill Sheffer.

"That's tough on Bob," Overton said sympathetically. "This team is death on southpaws. Rick and I found that out right off the bat."

"Bill's fast," Chip said calmly. "He'll take care of them."

Sheffer took care of them, just as Chip said he would. Pitching like a big-league fireman, he struck out the first man he faced and forced the next hitter to send a weak ground ball to Brett Degnan, who fielded it cleanly and made the sure play at first for the second out. The runner on third scampered home, making it Plainsmen 5, Yankees 3.

That left two on, runners on second and third, and two away. But Sheffer was the master. He kept ahead of the Yankee hitter and won the game himself by fielding a high hopper and making the sure throw to Biggie Cohen for the third out and the game.

Biggie stomped the sack with his size-fourteen spikes and headed for the dugout to give Bill Sheffer a southpaw slap on the back with his hamlike hand and to shove the ball into his glove.

"Try that in your trophy case, Bill," Biggie said happily. "Man, you earned it!"

NUMBER ONE!

Chip and Ken Overton got there just in time to join the whole team giving Sheffer a cheer, and then the Plainsmen rushed for the locker room. Soapy voiced their thoughts. "Now for the Miners and the championship!"

That would have been enough baseball in one day for most people. It was for most of the Plainsmen. But it wasn't enough for Chip Hilton, Biggie Cohen, and Soapy Smith. They'd caught the fervent baseball fever gripping Parkville, and right after dinner, they started for Bear Stadium to watch a minor league game.

The Midwestern League is composed of eight clubs, each one under the umbrella of a major league organization. Although the minor league rosters contain a few older players nearly past their peak, most of the players are hustling youngsters, rookies, and other hopefuls who are being tested and primed for big-league action. This year the race was developing into a dogfight between the Parkville Bears and the Hedgetown Raptors. The game tonight was an important one, and each manager was starting his best pitcher. Eddie Duer had named Scissors Kildane as the Bears' starting pitcher, and Boots Rines had elected to go with Lefty Turner, the pride of the Raptors.

Chip could hardly wait for the tall hurler to start the game. He studied the Bears lineup on the scoreboard in center field and listened to the enthusiastic Parkville fans as they talked about their favorite players.

"Eddie's starting his strongest club. Wants to win this one bad."

"Eddie wants to win 'em all!"

"Just look at that lineup and tell me what's holdin' 'em up. The only player with any real experience is Curry."

"You know why Mickey Curry's here, don't you?"

"Sure, because the Drakes want an experienced catcher handling Eddie's rookie pitchers."

"Well, wouldn't you want an old hand behind the plate to develop surefire big-leaguers like Kildane and Akers?"

"What's wrong with Richards and Mills?"

"Oh, Richard's too small. Besides, he doesn't throw that hard."

"Mills throws a mean fastball!"

"Sure, but where? He's just as liable to throw it over the grandstand as over the plate."

"All lefties are like that if they're fast!"

"Phil Akers isn't a lefty, and he's sure wild enough."

"He's not really wild! And even if he is, his wildness helps him more than it hurts him. Hitters don't dig in at the plate when he's pitching."

"Me, I like Kildane!"

"Who doesn't?"

Chip studied the batting order of the Bears and compared the lineup with his program. Corky Squill, the leadoff hitter, was listed as five-nine and weighing 180 pounds. Damon Boyd, the "push-along" shortstop, was listed precisely the same. Chip glanced at the infield. The double-play combination looked exactly like twins from where he sat. Bill Dawson, batting third and playing left field, was listed at an even six feet and 190 pounds.

The cleanup hitter was Alan "Stretch" Johnson. It was easy to see where Johnson got his nickname. The tall first baseman seemed all arms but didn't look as though he weighed even 185 pounds! Chip's guess was that Johnson was about as tall as Biggie.

Chip shifted his eyes to the outfield again. Norm Klein in center field and Ted Smith in right were each listed at six-one and 195. They moved fast and had good arms.

NUMBER ONE!

Third base was patrolled by a short, aggressive player who gunned the ball across to Stretch Johnson on a string. Chip studied Paul Hale intently. He'd heard a lot about Hale. He was five-ten and weighed only 160 pounds, but he was already tabbed as a future Golden Glove winner.

Then Chip focused on the catcher, Mickey Curry. The burly receiver batted in the eighth spot and captained the team. He was listed as six-two, 210 pounds, and he had an arm that was *an arm*!

Soapy followed Chip's glance and then elbowed Biggie. "Ever see anyone throw like that?" he demanded.

Biggie shook his head. "Nope," he smiled in admiration, "I've never seen anyone throw like that, and I don't see how they can keep him out of the majors."

"Bats .380, says here," Soapy added.

The announcer's voice echoed through the stadium asking everyone to stand as the Bears and the Raptors lined up in front of their dugouts and the soloist began singing "The Star Spangled Banner."

A minute later, the plate umpire held up his hands and announced the batteries, and the Bears trotted out to their positions. Kildane was last out of the dugout, and every Parkville fan leaped to his feet in tribute to the Bears' great hurler.

"Go, Kildane!"

"Cut 'em up, Scissors!"

"Come on, you Bears!"

Kildane was fast, as fast as lightning. His long throwing arm reached nearly to the ground when he pointed his left toe toward third base. When he pivoted around and took his stride, he seemed to reach right across the plate.

Butch Bates led off for the Raptors, crowding the plate, looking for a free ride. But he didn't have a chance.

Kildane's fastball darted down across the plate three straight times, and the disappointed shortstop was called out on strikes. Sandy Adams and Nick Marreno quickly followed. Three up and three down and the crowd cheered Kildane every step of the way to the dugout. Chip, Soapy, and Biggie cheered right to the last too.

Corky Squill, the Bears' chunky second baseman, led off for the home team. On the first pitch he electrified everyone in the stadium by banging a three-bagger to right center. Lefty Turner, the Raptors' number one pitcher, didn't like that and added to his woes by walking Damon Boyd.

Bill Dawson was up, and the eager left fielder brought the home crowd to its feet again by doubling off the right-field wall, giving the Bears two quick runs. Turner settled down then, struck out Johnson and Klein, and forced Ted Smith to fly out to Bo Roth in left field.

Scissors Kildane's mastery over the Raptors held. The big man seemed tireless, and as inning after inning passed, he continued to control the hitters. Lefty Turner never recovered from his bad start. Two hours and twenty minutes later, the Bears had won by a score of 6-1 and had increased their lead in the win column by three games, with two less defeats in the important loss column.

Chip was glad the Bears had won. He admired Scissors Kildane's quiet confidence and baseball prowess. The Raptors, on the other hand, had turned out to be sore losers. Lefty Turner had used a vicious duster, forcing the Bears hitters to back away from the plate all through the game. Chip could understand a pitcher moving back a batter who crowded the plate or got out of the batter's box, but to aim the ball deliberately at an opposing player's head was poor sportsmanship. Turner was a sullen and vicious player, and Chip was glad he had lost.

NUMBER ONE!

Chip grinned, though, when he thought about Corky Squill. In the field he was like ice water; he never batted an eyelash or made any unnecessary move after he got into his position. When Turner had dusted Corky off, the stocky second baseman had charged out to the mound waving his bat and had chased the Raptors' pitching star clear back to second base.

Later that night, when the lights were out and Chip was trying to go to sleep, he was still thinking about the game and about the Bears. Maybe someday he could be a pitcher like Scissors Kildane . . . maybe after college . . . maybe . . .

The next afternoon Chip, Soapy, and Biggie were back in the same seats in the stadium and again they were pulling for the Bears. Realizing every game with the Bears was doubly important, the Raptors were clawing at them now, using every trick in the book. Once again, Corky Squill and Scissors Kildane came through.

Squill had another perfect day at bat, scoring two of the Bears' three runs himself and driving in the third. In the field he was brilliant, making four spectacular stops and teaming up with Damon Boyd and Stretch Johnson to complete three sensational double plays. Chip marveled at Squill's immobility in his position. Once he set himself, the stocky, bowlegged infielder seemed almost asleep; but when a play developed, he bolted into action.

In the top of the ninth, with the Bears leading 3-2 and two down, Troy Richards got into trouble. He hit Sandy Adams, walked Nick Marreno, and pitched himself into a two-and-nothing hole with Jack Castillo, the Raptors' cleanup hitter. Eddie Duer called time, and after a brief consultation on the mound with Richards, surprised everyone in the ballpark, except Scissors Kildane, when he called the big pitcher in from the bullpen. The crowd went wild.

"Kildane! He's gonna use Kildane!"

"I don't get it! Scissors worked yesterday!"

"Duer's crazy! He'll *ruin* the kid!"

"Shut up! Eddie knows what he's doing!"

Eddie Duer knew what he was doing all right. So did Scissors Kildane. The tall hurler didn't fool around. He breezed his warm-up pitches across the plate, waited until Castillo stepped up there, and then broke a curveball across the outside corner for a called strike.

Completely ignoring the base runners, Scissors fired the next pitch across Castillo's wrists. The Raptors slugger swung too late. The stadium was on its feet now, tense and tight and breathless as Kildane toed the rubber and took his stretch. Scissors was in control. He dropped his hands to his belt and held them there for a long second. Then Kildane twisted his body, kicked his long leg, pivoted with lightning speed, and released a knuckler.

Jack Castillo, trying to outguess Kildane, had expected a fast one and had started his swing. When he saw the knuckler, he slowed his bat and made a desperate effort to knock the dancing ball out of the park, but all his bat found was the breeze. Mickey Curry had the ball in his hip pocket and was on his way to the dugout before Castillo regained his balance. Dismayed, Castillo realized a single might have won the game. Yet he'd been caught anticipating, missed the ball by a mile, struck out with two aboard, and lost his chance to win the game.

The emotion-charged fans were on their way just as the ball smacked into Curry's glove. They spilled over the barriers and out onto the field, heading to congratulate Kildane. Their hero had won another game, and they wanted to show their appreciation.

The celebration didn't end on the field. That night, all over Parkville, people were talking about their team and about Scissors Kildane, Eddie Duer, Corky Squill, Mickey Curry, and Troy Richards.

Chip and his buddies went to their rooms early, determined to be rested and ready for the championship game. But downstairs in the lobby, in the restaurant, and around the pool, the scouts gathered and compared notes. Only Gabby Breen was missing.

Gabby liked to be secretive and dramatic, and he was eager to try his theatrics on Chip Hilton. His best prop was the mighty dollar. Since he believed the end justified the means, he was determined to ignore Eddie Duer's instructions about not approaching the All-Stars during the tournament. But Breen couldn't move without ready cash, and he was nearly frantic because the money hadn't arrived. Gabby had been on Rines's heels as soon as he'd left the locker room. Now he was badgering the manager in his room at the Park Hotel.

"Come on, what's the matter with you? You said I'd have the cash today! I gotta move fast! This kid's gonna be leaving here tomorrow, the draft is comin' up, and you'll miss out on him just like you missed out on Scissors Kildane."

"Listen, Gabby," Rines explained patiently, "I told you I sent your message. That's all I'm gonna do! Don't forget I'm managing a ball club, trying to win a pennant! I've got to concentrate on winning games!"

Breen's face was contorted and purple with anger. He could hardly restrain himself. "But this kid's for real!

You're actin' just like you did last year. Bullheaded! And that's why you're in second place and gettin' nowhere fast. If you'd listened to me last year, you woulda had Kildane, and you woulda been sittin' pretty for the top spot this year too! You're gonna keep foolin' around and end up without a job!"

"That's enough, Gabby!" Rines snapped. "I've done all I'm gonna do; the rest is up to Kearns. Good night!"

Breen stalked out of the room and headed straight for the nearest phone. Boots Rines probably didn't suspect it, but he had just incurred the bitter malice of an unscrupulous man, a man who was now determined to do everything in his power to undermine Rines with the owner of the Raptors, hoping to win the job for himself.

Yes, Gabby wanted Rines's job as manager of the Raptors, and he meant to get it. Boots had had his chance. Gabby Breen was looking out for number one!

CHAPTER 5

From the Heart

HUNTER KEARNS, successful real estate developer and owner of the minor league Hedgetown Raptors, usually believed in giving his manager a free hand in running the team. But financial considerations had to override his hands-off policy. He knew he had to take charge and do something now.

Hedgetown fans loved a winner, but they wouldn't support a loser. Hunter Kearns couldn't afford a losing ball club. Last year's success had gone to the heads of Hedgetown's fans. They couldn't understand why the Raptors, their champions, were trailing behind the Bears in second place. Especially since the Bears' roster was stacked with younger players and several rookies. Boots Rines, the manager of the Raptors, hadn't recommended any major changes in the player roster, and Hedgetown's fans had looked forward to a runaway race again this year. But when the Parkville Bears grabbed the top spot and held it, the fans became disgruntled and began looking for someone to blame.

DUGOUT JINX

Gabby Breen was clever and observant. He knew the Raptors followers were smoldering about losing, so he decided to fan the flames to his own advantage. His frequent conversations with spectators were diplomatically punctuated with off-hand remarks about Rines's "tough luck" in missing out on pursuing Scissors Kildane and Corky Squill in the off season when he'd had a chance. He always followed up by stating Rines was too easygoing with his players and didn't push them enough.

"You know," Breen would say hesitantly, "maybe I shouldn't be talkin' this way—and I sure wish Boots nothing but the best—but it might be the best thing that ever happened to Rines if Kearns gave him a rest. Now, this is strictly confidential, and I know you won't repeat it: Rines is losing his grip. He's all stressed out, and it's hurtin' the team. He's on the verge of a breakdown."

Some Hedgetown fans swallowed Breen's "confidential" information, and when the Bears continued to lead the division, the Raptors fans increased their demands for change. Boots Rines inevitably became the scapegoat the fans had been seeking.

Hunter Kearns knew something had to be done before the fans showed their lack of support by staying away from the park, which he couldn't afford. He'd tried to appease the fans and assure the skeptical sportswriters who expressed their doubts about the manager's ability to get the job done, but his support of Rines merely added fuel to the fervor.

Pressure from the fans and sportswriters had mounted after a double loss to the Bears—forcing a showdown. Hunter Kearns was worried—about his real estate developments and now about his club. Gabby Breen's early morning phone call only fired his temper further.

"Hilton?" Kearns repeated testily. "Never heard of him! What fax? No, I haven't heard from Boots. You mean better than Kildane? Alright, relax, tell me."

An impatient Hunter Kearns doodled on his desk pad as he half listened to Breen and then interrupted, "Gabby, you know as well as I do that our parent organization decides who to select in the draft, and they've spent weeks preparing for it. I'd be sticking my neck way out if I recommended they change their top pick to this Hilton kid just before the draft. We're in a slump, and I certainly don't need heat from the head office. I've already got the writers and fans on my back."

Gabby's voice trembled with excitement. "Mr. Kearns, I *assure* you that I can deliver Chip Hilton to the Raptors! I've nosed around. The word is, the kid won't be drafted. His high school coach told everybody he's going to college to follow in dear old dad's footsteps. I hear the kid even told Stu Gardner the same thing. So, nobody's going to waste a draft pick on him."

Kearns shot back, "Then why should we be the dummies and waste one?"

Gabby repeated his earlier statement, "Mr. Kearns, I *assure* you that I can deliver Chip Hilton to the Raptors!

"I've got a plan that'll give him no choice but to be wearin' a Raptors uniform before you know it! The press and fans'll eat it up! But I need some cash, and you gotta be ready to make that recommendation. You might even get a special two-for-one deal. Remember what I said about Kildane," Breen gloated.

Hunter Kearns sighed, "I know all about Kildane. All I've heard from you all year has been Kildane and Squill, Squill and Kildane! Never mind all that. You'd better get back here next Thursday or Friday. I might have to do something about Eddie before the team comes home. You think you could take charge starting with our game here with the Bears? . . . There isn't anyone else and you know it! . . . That's better! Naturally, I want Boots to finish out the season. But if he keeps losing, I'll have to do something about it. . . . All right, you be ready! But don't breathe a word of this to anyone. Understand? I might not have to let him go. . . . Good. I'll be expecting you Thursday or Friday at the latest. . . . Yes, I'll send what I can."

Gabby Breen hung up and stood motionless in the phone booth. He was afraid he'd wake up and find it was all a dream. Kearns was all but offering him Rines's job. By this time next week, he might be the manager of the Raptors. He would be for sure if they kept losing.

While Gabby Breen had been making his call, Chip was making his to Valley Falls. Mary Hilton was glad to find out that Chip was all right and she wanted to hear all about the tournament. Many teenagers feign annoyance when their parents worry about them, although they really like it. Chip was concerned about his mom and her happiness, and he wouldn't have dreamed of enjoying a success without sharing it with her.

Chip was thinking about his mom all through Pat Reynolds's strategy session later that morning, and she was in his thoughts when he was introduced and stepped out in front of the dugout that afternoon beside his Plainsmen teammates.

When "The Star Spangled Banner" filled the air, Chip took off his cap, holding it in front of the letters on his baseball jersey. He looked steadily at the flag waving so proudly above the scoreboard in center field. Before he realized it, he had finished his warm-up pitches and was standing behind the mound, looking down the alley at Soapy. Biggie's booming "Pour it on 'em, Chipper" made him feel strong and ready, and he pulled his cap a little lower over his left eye and toed the rubber.

Chip had been just another high school pitcher to Parkville baseball fans a few days ago—before his opening game no-hitter. That performance had endeared him to the baseball enthusiasts, and the thunderous cheer greeting him now came from the heart.

Gabby Breen watched the other scouts closely, and when he saw their intent interest in the young hurler, he began to berate Boots Rines under his breath. His anger provided his willing conscience full justification for going after Rines's job. Suddenly his thoughts were interrupted by the talk of the surrounding fans.

"Best young pitcher I ever saw!"

"You can say that again! He's ready for this league right now!"

"Wonder how early a kid like that will go in the draft?"

Gabby Breen was perspiring freely now, and his waxen complexion had turned pink. He was worried. What if Hilton was drafted by another team? His glance shot toward the Plainsmen dugout, and his eyes narrowed as they focused on Stu Gardner. A tremendous cheer from the crowd drew his eyes back to the field, and he nudged the fan on his right. "What happened?" he asked.

"What's the matter with you? You blind? That's the kid's second straight strikeout. Two up and two down, just like that!"

The third hitter grounded weakly to Rico White. The little shortstop scooped up the ball, and his underhand throw beat the runner by twenty feet. The crowd gave Chip another hand, and he lifted his cap awkwardly as he ducked into the friendly, familiar refuge of the dugout.

DUGOUT JINX

Just the same, the Miners weren't knuckling down to the Plainsmen. Even though they couldn't get to Chip Hilton, they fought tenaciously and won the crowd's admiration for their brilliant defensive play. But the Plainsmen had too much power, and little by little the Miners began to cave in.

Chip felt stronger every inning. Going into the top of the eighth, with the Plainsmen leading 3-0, he had another no-hitter on the fire. Then, as often happens, Chip's teammates began to pull for the perfect game and unconsciously tightened up in their play. Suddenly, for the first time, Chip realized that no Miners had reached first base, and he, too, began to feel the pressure. With two down, he got behind the hitter with a three-and-nothing count.

Pat Reynolds wisely took charge. "Time!" he yelled from the top of the dugout steps. He recognized those familiar symptoms and substituted Ken Overton for Soapy Smith.

Chip realized Reynolds was sparring for time, giving him a chance to settle down. The crowd knew it too. The fans were tense, pulling for the tall, gray-eyed pitcher from Valley Falls.

The plate umpire allowed Chip five pitches to Overton and then called, "Play ball!" There was a heavy hush over the stadium as Chip took a full windup and threw his fastball right across the middle of the plate for a called strike. Chip could almost feel the crowd's tension lift for a brief moment. Then it came right back.

Chip toed the rubber and sent another fastball toward Overton's target, but the ball never reached Overton. The batter smacked it just right, full on the nose! Chip saw the blur of the ball as it shot out and up like a streak of lightning over third base and headed for left field. He turned, slow motion, to watch the flight of the ball.

Then he focused on Gabe Mariani's twinkling legs. Gabe wasn't even looking at the ball. He was heading at full speed for the extreme left corner of the field where the white chalked foul line met the fence. Mariani leaped high in the air, made a backhand stab at the ball, and crashed into the fence. The crash was heard all over the field. But even as he fell, a triumphant Mariani held the captured ball aloft.

The third-base umpire, on top of the play, had followed the ball into the outfield and jerked his thumb high in the air for the out. The umpire's signal seemed to release the crowd from mass hypnosis.

The roar that followed almost shook the stands off their foundations. Gabe Mariani's catch was the third out, but the determined left fielder was out too! The wind was knocked right out of him! The umpire called time and signaled for the team's trainer.

The crowd stood in hushed silence as she kneeled over the fallen player. A few long minutes later, a groggy Gabe regained his breath. Chip and Biggie, each with one of Mariani's arms draped over a shoulder, led him to the dugout. The cheering became one continuous roar.

The Plainsmen scored another run in the bottom of the eighth to make the score 4-0. In the end, the run wasn't needed, and the Plainsmen didn't even need their last time at bat. Chip set the Miners down one, two, three to win the championship, hurling a perfect game— no hits, no walks, and sixteen strikeouts!

The Parkville fans gave Chip the Kildane treatment then, swarming out on the field and lifting him up on top of the dugout. They cheered until they had all of the

Plainsmen up there. Next to Chip, Gabe Mariani got the biggest ovation. It took the Plainsmen half an hour to get to their locker room. They weren't complaining however; they were the champs, and they loved it!

At the tournament banquet that evening, a still jubilant Soapy Smith reminded Scissors Kildane about his earlier prediction. "We killed 'em! We killed 'em!" he hooted. Biggie frowned and elbowed Soapy's ribs, motioning to the dais where Pat Reynolds was speaking.

"I'm sure the players will always appreciate their tournament watches, All-Star jackets, and team photos. But I'm sure they will treasure even more Parkville's wonderful hospitality. The Bears fans really love their baseball! As the coach of the Plainsmen, I've been very privileged to work with such a fine group of young men. I shall always cherish this experience as one of the highlights of my coaching career."

Pat Reynolds received a tremendous ovation, and then the emcee introduced William Malloy, the proud owner of the Bears.

"This night culminates one of the most enjoyable weeks of my life. I think the only possible rival to this occasion will be the night we win this year's pennant—"

Malloy was drowned out by the cheering, the clanging of silverware on glasses, and the banging of fists on tables, which threatened to break every piece of china in the room. When the enthusiasm finally subsided, Malloy continued.

"Now, it's my privilege to announce the name of the most valuable player—"

"Hilton! Chip Hilton!" Cries came from all over the banquet hall.

"We want Hilton! We want Hilton!"

It took longer for the speaker to gain quiet this time. Chip's face was scarlet, and his hands toyed nervously with his program.

"There's absolutely no doubt about the choice nor the worthiness of the honor. William "Chip" Hilton, it is my pleasure to present you with this plaque certifying your unanimous selection by the All-Star coaches, sportswriters, and members of the Parkville tournament committee as the most valuable player in the tournament.

"Furthermore, we'd like to keep you around Parkville a little longer. We have a summer intern position available in our baseball operation, and we'd like you to fill that spot. Additionally, our manager, Eddie Duer, has asked if you'd like to become a special bench guest of the Bears for the balance of the season."

"Speech! We want Hilton! Speech!"

Chip got to his feet somehow and waited until the applause subsided. He felt a tightness in his chest, and the words he spoke were in the voice of a stranger, hollow and far away.

"Thank you, Mr. Malloy. I deeply appreciate this honor. I also want to express my thanks to Coach Reynolds and all my teammates. It's great to be a member of the championship team, playing on the same team with so many All-Stars who are so much more deserving of this award than I am."

Chip sat down, almost overwhelmed by his feelings toward his teammates. He just couldn't understand why he couldn't put his thoughts into more eloquent phrases.

He didn't need to worry. Every person in the room knew what Chip meant. His sincerity and humility were like magic—simple words that caught their hearts.

Later, when the crowd filtered into the Park Hotel lobby, Soapy and Biggie talked excitedly about the internship. The two friends were proud of their team-mate. They knew how hard he'd worked all through high school and how much the award meant to him. Chip, however, was thinking about someone else—his mom, Mary Hilton. Chip had wanted to spend as much time as possible with her before he started at State.

"You could come home the last week, Chip," Biggie said. "Football camp doesn't open until August. You could stay with the Bears most of the season and still have a week at home."

Chip remained uncertain. Scissors Kildane saw the worry on Chip's face and joined the three friends.

"Congratulations, Mr. MVP! You're coming with us, aren't you?" Then Kildane answered his own question. "Of course you are! You'll learn a lot of baseball, and I'll help you with your pitching. Not that I know any more than your coach, but I can teach you some of the things I had to learn the hard way. Besides, you'll be in on the hottest baseball race in the country. The Raptors beat the Knights today, 8-1. Looks like it will be a dogfight all season long. You'd better stick around, Chip. What do you say?"

"I'll talk it over with my mom," Chip said hesitantly.

"Good!" Kildane said enthusiastically. "Come on! We'll call her right now from your room! Let me talk to her! I'd like to give her the news!"

Mary Hilton listened to Scissors Kildane's effervescent recounting of the championship game and the internship.

"Of course he can stay, if he wants," Mary asserted. "What does Chip want? May I talk to him?"

While Chip was trying to talk to his mom, Soapy, Biggie, and Kildane were pummeling Chip and one another with pillows in celebration.

Chip tried to talk above the clamor. "Yes, I think it's a great opportunity too, and I'd like to do it. These guys are going crazy, Mom," he laughed. "Absolutely crazy! But, I like it!"

The next afternoon Chip and his teammates sat in a special box behind the Parkville dugout and watched the Bears beat the Panthers 2-1 in a tight pitchers' duel. However, when the game was over and his teammates and friends left for home, Chip waited alone, just a bit lonesome. Finally Kildane came hustling up, fresh from his shower, and hurried Chip out to the yellow sports car in the parking lot.

"Come on, Chip," Kildane said happily, "we're having dinner with the guys. You're going to see how the other half lives."

Another car trailed not far behind the yellow convertible. Gabby Breen chuckled softly to himself. He'd have the money first thing in the morning. Meanwhile, William "Chip" Hilton wasn't getting out of his sight!

CHAPTER 6

Promises, Promises, Promises

GABBY BREEN finally received his express letter early Monday morning and promptly slid the cashier's check across the counter to the teller at the Parkville National Bank.

"Make it all tens," he said loftily.

The teller's eyes opened wide in amazement as she scanned the piece of paper. "All in twenty-dollar bills?" she echoed.

"That's what I said!"

"Do you have an account with us? May I please see two forms of identification? This may take a few minutes."

"Don't think I need an account since this is a cashiers check, and I'll wait," Breen said carelessly.

Twenty minutes later, the teller watched the over-dressed man saunter happily away from the counter and out the door, nonchalantly swinging his filled briefcase.

Breen was in a jovial mood. He had the money now, and he wasn't worrying about Chip Hilton as long as he was in Eddie Duer's care. No, Duer wouldn't attempt to influence the kid as long as he was with the Bears. But that didn't mean Gabby Breen wasn't going to take advantage of every opportunity that came his way.

Meanwhile, he'd check out the Bears and hope the Raptors lost the next three games. First thing on the list, though, was to get acquainted with the kid. "The sooner the better," he warned himself. "If I can sign Hilton, that Cohen kid will follow. It's like getting two for the price of one. I'd better use Corky to set Hilton up for a meeting. Gardner will probably head out for that hick town and wait for the kid to come home. Well, good ole Gabby Breen will have Chip Hilton signed, sealed, and delivered long before that."

Chip was fighting pangs of homesickness when he came down to breakfast, but they quickly disappeared when he saw Scissors waiting in the lobby. Kildane was standing by the front desk, talking baseball with the clerk. When he saw Chip, he came striding forward, his customary smile lighting his gray-green eyes.

"Thought you were going to sleep all morning," Kildane chided good-naturedly. "You're in fast company now, Chipper, and you have to get up early to be ahead of the pack. C'mon. I'll keep you company while you have breakfast. I talked with Mr. Malloy this morning, and he agreed to assign you to Eddie Duer for part of your internship. Eddie might let you toss a few at batting practice this morning. We hit at eleven, and you'll need a uniform. A Bears uniform!"

After breakfast, Kildane drove swiftly to the ballpark and led Chip into the clubhouse. He introduced him to the trainer, a cheerful man, about fifty, who greeted Scissors with a wide grin of affection and then gripped Chip's hand with a friendly pressure.

"Hi, Chip. I'm Roy Potts," he said warmly, "but the boys call me Pepper. You can do the same. Now, come on over here and let me get you some working clothes."

The room was filled with Bears players, dressing slowly and idly kidding one another about their hitting, their weight, their girlfriends or wives, and anything else that came to mind. Yet all the while there was an undercurrent of grim purpose in the room, and Chip sensed that the pressure was beginning to show. The Bears had led the league since the opening week of the season, but the pressure had never let up; they couldn't seem to get a commanding lead.

After Chip was dressed in the Bears uniform, Kildane introduced him to every player in the room. Chip remembered some of them from the three games he'd seen, but they looked entirely different close up. Mickey Curry, the powerful catcher with the long arms and the peg to the bases that had earned him the respect of every base runner in the league, seemed completely different as Chip stood next to him. His face was gentle, he spoke softly, and his smile was tender and friendly.

Pete Mills, the lefty hurler who was tagged with the nickname Windy, seemed to have the same personality off the field as he had on the mound. Now, Chip knew how he got his name—the voluble pitcher never stopped talking.

"This is Stretch Johnson, Chip," Kildane continued, "the best first baseman in the league."

The tall player was about six-three and his arms seemed as long as Scissors's as he extended his hand to Chip, laughing and winking. "Kildane's a great kidder, Chip," he said lightly. "Better watch him."

It was easy to see why Scissors Kildane was the most popular player on the Bears team. The big athlete always boosted his teammates, praising them all the time. Chip had only known Kildane a week, but he'd never heard him make a negative remark about anyone during that time.

Chip felt a surge of gratitude as he thought of the genuine interest the tall pitcher had taken in him. From the other players' warm reception, it was obvious Kildane was more than just popular; he was a loyal friend and respected leader.

"Shake hands with Corky Squill, Chip. He's our lead-off hitter and the best in the business."

Chip had watched Squill work in the Raptors games, and he agreed that Squill was a good second baseman. The keystone guardian didn't look five-nine, nor did he look as though he weighed 180 pounds. Chip got the uncomfortable feeling that Corky Squill was the type of player who made enemies easily and liked it. He was quick-tempered, and Chip had noted that Squill had been extremely careless with his spikes on the bases.

In the field, Squill was noncommunicative, totally different from what one expected in a second baseman. Usually they were "holler" players who spark the team, keeping them pumped and enthusiastic. Squill, however, never said a word when he was on the field. In fact, during the three games Chip had watched, Corky had stood so quietly in his position and moved so imperceptibly that Chip couldn't figure how he managed to get into position to field the ball. But he did, every time.

"Glad to meet you, Hilton," Squill said briefly, extending a limp hand. As soon as Chip released his hand, Squill turned away.

Lastly, Kildane introduced Coach Bob Reiter; Paul Hale, the third baseman; and the Bears' outfielders: Bill Dawson, Norman Klein, and Ted Smith. Their conversation was cut short when Eddie Duer called for the team's attention.

Chip studied the manager as he addressed his players. Eddie Duer was, Chip judged, about forty years old, six feet tall, and weighed about 180 pounds. His movements were quick, and his steady black eyes were keen and bright. The prominent nose that had earned him the nickname "Eagle" was set above a small, thin-lipped mouth, and his face was deeply tanned. Duer looked fit. His voice was sharp, and he spoke decisively and forcefully.

"We've got to start hitting. We're getting the pitching, but we're going to run into trouble if we can't get more runs. We all know the pitching staff is overworked, but that can't be helped. Whitey's arm is in bad shape, so Scissors, Windy, Troy, and Phil will have to carry the load. They can do it, too, but they have to have some runs. The close games are the killers because the pitcher can't let up; he has to bear down all the way.

"We've got to get the wins from the rest of the league and do no worse than hold our own with the Raptors. Now, I want you men to remember that the next several weeks mean everything; every game is important, and every hit and every throw is vital. Pitchers, every batter you face is up there ready to knock the juice out of it every time he looks at the apple. We've got a chance to turn up the heat on the rest of the league. It's up to us to set the pace."

Duer paused and nodded in Chip's direction. "I guess most of you have met Chip Hilton, who won the MVP award in the high school All-Star tournament. I want to welcome him officially and let him know that as long as he's a summer intern with us, he's considered a member of the Bears organization. Chip, I know the team joins me in welcoming you as one of the guys." There was a burst of applause, and then Duer continued.

"Now let's go out and get some more batting practice. Hilton, you can throw a few as soon as you finish with Pepper."

Chip was pumped as he warmed up. When he walked out beside the mound and started pouring controlled pitches across the plate, he was shaking from excitement. This was incredible! He was serving them up for minor-league players in a regular ballpark. But Chip didn't try anything fancy. He didn't smoke his fastball across the plate. He simply concentrated on his control, placing the ball where the hitters could meet it solidly.

Up in the stands, Gabby Breen sat in the same seat he'd occupied for the past week. Some of his friendly Bears fans were there too. Breen watched the tall blond youth whip the ball effortlessly across the plate and pointed out the important pitching traits Chip possessed.

"Watch that pivot! Smooth, eh? You can tell a real pitcher by his pivot and his stride. The kid's got a nice, easy stride and a perfect finish."

"You must like him," someone remarked.

"I do and I don't," Breen said appraisingly. "Lots of kids have form, but they gotta have that fastball, the change-up, and good control to make it in the big time."

"Looks like a great prospect to me," a fan said firmly. "He showed a lot of stuff setting those kids on their ears last Saturday."

"Yeah," another fan added, "he didn't give up a hit in eighteen innings. Personally, I think he'll go in the first round of the draft."

Breen didn't do much talking after the game started. He was thinking about the briefcase locked in the hotel safe and how he was going to approach Chip Hilton. He'd managed to do considerable scouting of the Bears too. Breen figured he'd need a lot of help if he got Boots Rines's job. Above all, he'd have to win those games against the Bears.

He smiled as he thought about his conversation with Hunter Kearns. By this time next week, he might be managing the Raptors. What a break! It was true that Boots had given him a chance when he needed it, but baseball was like any other business—a man couldn't let sentiment get in the way.

All in all, Boots Rines hadn't delivered, and if he lost the manager's spot, it was his own fault. The man was a chump. He should've pursued the guys Breen suggested, even if it did require a little bending of the rules. Well, Breen wouldn't make that mistake once he got to be skipper of the Raptors. He knew how to get the players he needed.

Breen glanced at Squill. He would need Corky if he got to be the manager of the Raptors. He focused his eyes on the chunky infielder. He'd taught that kid a lot, had corrected his faults, and got him into pro ball.

Even after Squill had made the Parkville team, Breen had worked with him, made suggestions about his style of play, and stayed close to the aggressive little infielder. Breen's forehead suddenly wrinkled, forming two deep frown lines between his eyebrows. His close-set eyes narrowed and a sly smile cracked his lips as he watched Squill's immobile figure. "That's it," he muttered, "that's it! Now to go to work on him."

The Bears had an easy time that afternoon. Scissors Kildane was ahead of the Panthers all the way, and the Parkville fans were thrilled as their heroes chalked up another win, 7-1. Chip was thrilled too. He was getting his first introduction to inside professional baseball.

PROMISES, PROMISES, PROMISES

Eddie Duer explained the signs between the catcher and the keystone combination.

"Curry gives the signs, Chip, and, unless the pitcher shakes him off, Corky and Damon flash 'em on to the rest of the team. That way, every player on the field knows what pitch is coming and knows just about where a batted ball should go. We chart where every opposing batter hits the ball against our pitchers.

"Signs aren't infallible of course—especially if the hitter's timing is bad, or if he swings too early or too late or checks his swing or changes his stance. The ball doesn't always go where we expect it, but at least knowing the kind of pitch helps us anticipate the ball's probable direction."

Duer confided that the Bears used three sets of signs that were changed frequently, sometimes in the same game. "Coaches can steal a team's signs, so we have to be careful," he added.

The Bears didn't need their last hits, and Chip waited for Scissors after the third out in the top of the ninth. Eddie Duer waited too.

"That's it, Scissors," Duer said decisively. "That's all the pitching you're doing for another week. You, my long-legged friend, are going to take a rest!"

"A rest?"

"That's what I said. A rest! We're going to need you for the whole season, so you're taking a little vacation."

"You mean I'm leaving the team? You're sending me down?"

"Of course not! It's nothing like that, but you're leaving the pitching to the rest of the guys for a week."

Kildane shook his head obstinately. "No way, Skipper. I'm taking my turn. I don't need a rest."

"I say you need a rest, and that's that!" Duer said firmly.

Kildane accepted the manager's decision without further argument, but he wasn't sold on the idea. "Don't understand it," he said lamely. "I never felt better in my life. Guess Eddie knows what he's doing, but I'd rather take my turn. I've got a rubber arm. I could pitch every day."

Stu Gardner was waiting at the hotel when Scissors and Chip arrived, and the scout joined them for dinner. He confided that he was leaving town and told Chip he'd probably see him play the following spring at State.

"You'll like it up there, Chip," he said enthusiastically. "It's a great school, and you're fortunate to have the opportunity to go there. You know the first-year player draft is in a few days, and my organization, the Drakes, is interested in you and Biggie. If we thought there was a chance either you or Biggie would play for us, we'd put both of you at the top of our draft selections.

"But you, Biggie, and Henry Rockwell have been honest with us and adamant about State, and we'll respect your decision. Don't let anyone talk you out of your resolve to go to college, no matter how attractive the proposition might seem now. Remember, you'll still have the same opportunity when you finish college, and you'll be a better pitcher. Am I right, Scissors?"

Kildane nodded soberly. "He sure is, Chip. I wish someone like Stu had talked to me when I got out of high school. My coach and my parents tried to get me to go on, but like most kids, I thought I knew it all. I've been treated great by the Bears, but life for lots of guys in the minor leagues can be dismal—low pay, endless road trips, and lots of hard work. Yep, Stu's plenty right, Chip. You'll have lots of time to play ball after you earn your degree. I didn't get many offers, but you'll be getting them, Chip. And some of them might be hard to turn down."

PROMISES, PROMISES, PROMISES

"There's no doubt about that," Gardner agreed. "Some people will tell a youngster anything to get him signed to a contract. Often, there are more promises than reality. Some might tell you that it's all right to sign a contract and then go on to college and play ball. Any athlete would know that wasn't right if he took time to think it over, but they don't give you a chance. An athlete who signs a baseball contract becomes a professional as soon as he signs, and all the talk in the world won't change that fact.

"Well, I've got to be in Cleveland tomorrow to get ready for the draft. Chip, give my best to Coach Rockwell and your mom. Scissors, I'll be pulling for you down the stretch. Take good care of Chip."

Chip and Kildane stood at the curb a long time after Gardner's car had disappeared. As they drove to the movie theater at the mall, they talked about the friendly scout. Both agreed Stu Gardner was a fine man and a real baseball professional.

Gabby Breen had watched the meeting between Gardner and the two pitchers and he kept them in view all through dinner. Afterwards, he followed Chip and Scissors as far as the theater and then set out to meet Corky Squill.

Breen and Squill were seated at opposite ends of a bench in the Parkville Mall, each pretending to pass the time by reading the *Sporting News*. Gabby Breen knew the league rules prohibiting interclub fraternizing and so did Corky Squill. That was the reason they were so cautious in their meetings.

"Hear anything about the Hilton kid going with the team?" Breen asked.

"Sure. He's goin' with us."

"Think you guys are gonna draft him?"

"Nope, I don't think so. He's goin' to college, the way I hear it."

Breen smiled grimly. He'd have something to say about that after he'd shown the kid and his mother all that easy money.

Breen changed the subject. "I hear you and Eddie ain't been hittin' it off too good," he suggested.

"We get along good enough. Except when he starts gripin' when I throw the spikes a little. Heck with that!"

Breen nodded. "Corky, I've got news for you. Boots is on his way out!"

Squill was incredulous. "What? After winnin' the pennant last year? At this time of the season? You're making it up!"

Breen shook his head in mock sympathy for Rines. "Poor guy," he sighed. "Front office is coming down on him. They're sore because we can't knock you guys off. You know how they hate to lose to Parkville."

Squill chuckled. "I know. No doubt about that. We just own you guys, that's all."

"Listen, Corky, we got three games before we take you guys on in Hedgetown. Two with the Lions and one with the Panthers. If Boots doesn't win those three games, the press and the fans in Hedgetown will tear the park down. Another thing, if Boots goes, Gabby Breen moves in." The magazine he was holding hid Breen's twisted smile.

"You mean as manager? Really? As the skipper?"

"That's right! Sure as we're sittin' here. Kearns told me that over the phone last night." Breen leaned back, smirking, basking luxuriously in his own words.

There was a deep silence as Squill thought about Breen's statement. Then Gabby threw another bombshell.

"Could you use an extra three, four thousand bucks?"

Squill grunted incredulously. "Sure! What do you think? How?"

"Easy. Arrange a meeting with me and that Hilton kid so I can get his signature on a contract."

"How could I do that?"

"Easy. All you gotta do is play up to him. Only you gotta work fast. Be his best buddy!"

"I can try."

Gabby Breen extended his hand. "OK," he said. "It's a deal!"

There was another brief silence, each man busy with his own thoughts.

"Corky, if I get to be the boss of the Raptors, you're comin' with me as my team captain!"

"No way, Gabby! What makes you think the Bears would sell my contract or trade me to a team in the same division? You're nuts!"

"Yeah? Not so nuts! If the Raptors win the pennant, Kearns will get me any player I want. As the manager of the Raptors, there'll be a big bonus, and I'll have full say on replacements. The first one'll be Corky Squill as my team captain—along with a big salary increase. How's that?"

An ugly expression spread across Squill's face, and his black eyes glittered dangerously. For a second his whole body expressed so much rage that Breen instinctively recoiled. Then Corky recovered his self-possession and sank back, but his words rang just as dangerously.

"Look, Gabby, if you think I'm gonna do something out of line for you or for anyone else you're crazy!"

Breen's voice was silky smooth as he calmed the agitated second baseman. "I'm not askin' you to get out of line, Corky. Look, maybe I'm lookin' too far ahead, but I just wanted to cut you in on any good luck that might be comin' my way. Maybe nothin' at all will happen."

Breen paused and then continued with studied care. "The Raptors are a pretty good bunch to work for. Hunter Kearns is a great guy, and the Hedgetown fans can't be beat. They'd go for you in a big way. Anyway, I didn't mean you had to do anything wrong. You play your best all the time. Nothin's wrong so long as you can do that, is there? But, I gotta sell you to Kearns as a leader and a hustler. That means you gotta change your style of play on the field. I'll give you the details on that later. Right now, my big interest is that Hilton kid."

CHAPTER 7

Shortcut to Fame

THE NEXT MORNING when Chip entered the Bears dressing room, Corky Squill was the first player to greet him.

"Hey, Chip," Squill said pleasantly. "You know, when you were throwin' yesterday, it was the first time I've had a good hittin' workout all year. Sure wish you were goin' to be with us all the way to the end. Are you sure you can't stay until the end of the season?"

Chip was surprised, but immediately warmed to the usually stoic little infielder. "No, Mr. Squill," he said, "I've got to—"

"Call me Corky," Squill growled good-naturedly, a wide grin on his face.

"All right, Corky," Chip said awkwardly. "I'll throw some to you this morning if it's all right with Mr. Duer."

"It'll be all right, Chip," Squill said, grinning. Minutes later Chip and Corky walked out to the field together and began warming up.

Squill was pleased with himself. He could already see that three-thousand-dollar deposit in his savings account.

"This is a no-brainer!" he muttered. "Gabby will pull that briefcase out and this kid will fall all over himself." Then Squill's face clouded; Gabby had signed him for almost nothing.

The second baseman knew he hadn't gotten a very good deal, but he was grateful for Breen's interest. He'd been a naïve kid with no future when Gabby took him under his wing and gave him a chance. What Corky didn't know, however, was that Breen had padded his own savings account with some of Corky's signing bonus from the Bears.

Before Chip walked behind the pitching screen to throw batting practice to Corky, they were already becoming friends. Corky could be extremely likable when he wanted, and Breen's money was an immediate incentive. Corky could use that three thousand dollars. His small monthly minor-league paycheck didn't go very far, and he was only paid from April through September. He asked Chip to spend part of the evening with him, and chuckled with glee to himself when Chip accepted.

"We'll talk some baseball over dinner and then grab a movie," Corky said enthusiastically. "OK?"

When the game started, Chip found himself beside Scissors Kildane in the dugout. The lanky pitcher was complaining good-naturedly, but still enough to show he didn't like being pampered. His remarks were directed toward Chip but were loud enough for Duer to hear.

"Won't even let me throw in the bullpen," Scissors grumbled. "Must be out of his mind. I've gotta throw every day. I've got that kind of an arm. I wanna play!"

If Eddie Duer heard Kildane, he didn't let it show. He did show that he knew what he was doing that afternoon by choosing Windy Mills to pitch. The talkative hurler limited the Hickory Hornets to three hits. At bat, the Bears were murderous. They chased three Hornets hurlers and fattened up their own averages by amassing a total of eighteen hits. The game was a 13-0 rout.

The Lions made the Bears' afternoon a complete success. As the Bears players and fans enjoyed their lopsided victory, they watched a pitchers' duel develop between the Raptors and the Lions. The long rows of zeros stretched across the scoreboard until the last of the ninth, when the Lion frame flashed a big three and brought a cheer from the stands.

Gabby Breen almost cheered too. He nearly gave himself away by joining the crowd's jubilant roar, but he caught himself, limiting his pleasure to a satisfied chuckle. After the first joyous cheer, Breen's grandstand seatmates began needling the Raptors scout.

"Looks like you guys will be lucky to end up in third place this year," someone scoffed.

"My kid's Little League team could beat the Lions," another fan added.

"Hey, Breen! Hey, Gabby!" a shrill voice piped. "You better get yourself a uniform. The Raptors are fallin' apart!"

Breen grinned and took the razzing in stride. The fans weren't making him mad by celebrating the Raptors' defeat. Gabby was doing a little mental celebrating of his own. Two to go, and maybe he *would* be wearing a uniform—a manager's uniform.

Scissors joined Corky and Chip at dinner that evening. Kildane had never seen his teammate in such high spirits. Long after Chip and Corky left for the movie, he was still trying to figure it out.

Although the teammates respected Squill's baseball skills, his wall of silence had erected a barrier few of them tried to overcome. The lone exception was Stretch Johnson, the Bears' big first baseman. Corky and Stretch were two of a kind—quiet, self-contained, and close-mouthed. Their similar dispositions were probably the reason for their friendship. At any rate, Stretch was the only Bears regular Corky seemed to care about.

Corky bought the tickets, overruling Chip's objections, but he good-naturedly agreed to let Chip buy the popcorn and drinks. They were scarcely seated when Corky hopped up.

"Chip, I forgot to check with Pepper. Got to let him know where we are. It's one of Duer's rules. I'd better call him! Be right back!"

Corky's fertile mind had manufactured that excuse on the spur of the moment. He wanted to call Gabby Breen and let him know the progress he was making with Chip Hilton. Breen was waiting for the call and was just as excited as Squill.

"Gabby? . . . It's Corky! Guess what? . . . Right! Right with me! And, now listen! The kid's plannin' to go home tomorrow and get some clothes and stuff and meet us again at Clearview. You better plan to bump into us tonight, somewhere . . . How about the Pancake Shoppe on West Boulevard? . . . Good! Around ten."

Gabby Breen was whistling softly to himself as he made his plans. Chip Hilton would have company when he went home the next day.

When Gabby bumped into the two later in the restaurant, he pretended Corky Squill and Chip Hilton were the last people in the world he expected to see.

"Hey, Corky! What are you doin' here?"

Squill's act was perfect too. Obviously, he hadn't seen Gabby Breen in years. "Gabby!" Squill exploded. "Come on, sit down. Oh, by the way, this is Chip. Chip Hilton."

Breen feigned surprise, but he didn't overplay his act. He gripped Chip's hand hard and looked the youngster up and down with approving eyes.

"You look bigger out there on the field. Saw you pitch the championship game. Congratulations!"

"Won the MVP award too," Squill said proudly.

Breen nodded. "Couldn't miss," he said. "Had to be, just had to be."

Chip was relieved when the conversation swung away from him. The next half hour was devoted to the Midwestern League race and especially to the Bears and the Raptors. Squill and Breen batted the conversation back and forth, and Chip listened.

Chip studied the scout's sallow face and shifty eyes. Despite himself, Chip couldn't help comparing him to Stu Gardner. Gabby Breen seemed a perfect example of the kind of baseball scout Stu Gardner had described as conniving and irresponsible. Still, Chip tried to be pleasant, concealing his thoughts as best he could.

Just before they left the restaurant, Squill mentioned that Chip was going home in the morning to see his mom while the Bears had a day off.

"What a coincidence," Breen said, laughing. "I'm going that way. I can give you a ride."

Suddenly Stu Gardner's warning resounded in Chip's ears. He didn't want to be obligated, however he couldn't compete with both Squill and Breen. In the end, he reluctantly accepted Breen's invitation.

Breen beamed. "We'll leave first thing in the morning, Chip. I'll pick you up at the hotel at eight o'clock."

The three-hundred-mile drive passed pleasantly. Breen was talkative enough to make Chip feel at ease and thoughtful enough to turn on the radio after lunch to the broadcast of the Raptors-Lions game at Clearview.

A strange feeling suddenly gripped Chip; for the first time he realized Gabby Breen and Corky Squill had violated the league fraternizing rule Stu Gardner had told him about. Players, managers, and scouts were prohibited from fraternizing, and he'd been present at the violation scarcely a day after Gardner had explained the ruling.

The Raptors were having trouble with the Lions, and the game went into extra innings. Breen was driving steadily, absorbed in the game, and Chip's thoughts had free reign. He now regretted accepting the ride. Still, Corky Squill had been so nice that it would have been embarrassing to refuse.

The Lions eventually won the game 2-1 as the travelers neared Valley Falls, and Gabby Breen's impetuous grunt of pleasure surprised Chip. The wily scout quickly covered up.

"Looks like the Bears are going to back in, Chip, if we keep losing—even if the Bears did drop one to Hickory today at Parkville."

"I guess every game's important now," Chip ventured.

"It sure is. If the Bears knock us off next Saturday and Sunday, they'll just about put us out of the race. By the way, Chip, are you interested in professional baseball?"

Chip shook his head. "No, Mr. Breen, not now. I'm going to college."

"Good for you! Takes a lot of money to go to college, doesn't it?"

"It sure does. I don't know whether I'll be able to make it or not, but I'm going to try."

"You know, Chip, I may be able to help you out. Of course I can't talk about that until you get home. What time do your parents get home from work?"

Chip explained that his dad had been killed in an industrial accident. His mom was a supervisor with the phone company and was usually home before six o'clock. "She doesn't know I'm coming home. Guess I'll surprise her."

Gabby Breen decided he'd surprise Mary Hilton too. *I'll have to work this quickly,* he thought. *The briefcase deal ought to be just the ticket. This kid doesn't want his widowed mother to work, and I'll play that up strong too. Maybe I'd better use the association angle since this kid is so set on going to college.*

A few minutes later the two were in Valley Falls, and Breen pulled into the driveway of 131 Beech Street, the Hilton home.

"I may not see you for a few days, Chip, but sometime soon I'd like to see your mother and talk to her about your future. Think it would be all right if I dropped around to see her in a week or so?"

Chip hesitated briefly and then politely consented. After the scout left, however, Chip berated himself for being so congenial. "I should have said no," he muttered.

Breen checked in at the Valley Falls Inn and spent the next few hours making his plans and arranging and rearranging the money in the briefcase. He deliberated a long time about the amount he should place in the case.

He finally decided on ten thousand dollars. "That ought to do it," he grunted. "Then I'll give Corky three thousand and put the other two thousand in the old bank account. Not a bad night's work."

At 9:30 Breen, glancing at himself in the mirror, announced, "It's show time!" and picked up the briefcase. Ten minutes later he rang the Hilton doorbell.

Mary Hilton looked at Chip in amusement. "How does Soapy always know when a cake is just about to come out of the oven?"

"That's our Soapy," Chip said as he hopped up. Hoops trailed after him down the hall. Chip was surprised to see Gabby Breen filling the doorway, but he recovered quickly and asked the scout into the house.

"Mom, this is Mr. Breen, the gentleman who drove me home today. He's a scout for the Hedgetown Raptors."

Breen started his performance, answering the unspoken question in Chip's eyes. "Had car trouble right after I left, Chip. Just got it back. Guess it's fate! You see, besides my work with the Raptors, I'm also associated with an important athletic group. They caught me on my cell phone as the car was being repaired, and you know what? They told me to stay right here and come see you, Mrs. Hilton."

Mary Hilton was as patient as she was skeptical. She gazed questioningly at the stranger, yet listened politely as Breen continued.

"Your son is a fine athlete, Mrs. Hilton, and the organization I represent is deeply interested in his future. It's our business to protect young athletes like him. That's why I'm here. My boss received a number of reports on William, especially since he won the Most Valuable Player award at Parkville. Chip is his number one player. I've got all the confidence in the world in my boss. He insisted that I talk to you while I was here.

"Baseball is big business, and every kid is entitled to the best representation he can get. That's where the organization that I represent comes in. Our Sports

Assurance Program specializes in protecting fine, talented young athletes like your son, William, from those big and small baseball interests that often try to exploit them.

"We've enrolled hundreds of baseball players in our association, and no family has ever regretted our help. Of course, we're very careful. Every player is evaluated, reevaluated, and cross-checked until we *know* he's a surefire big leaguer. We don't approach any young man unless we're sure of that, and we're sure about your young Billy here."

While the visitor was talking, Chip was studying Breen's card, trying to figure out what this visit was all about. Who were these people he was talking about? And "Billy"? He hadn't been called Billy by anyone since preschool.

The card was neat and businesslike, but the name of the association was unfamiliar. Chip was confused. Nothing he had learned from Stu Gardner seemed to cover this situation.

"Since our organization is not directly tied to a specific team or any other baseball organization," Breen continued, "salary contracts, bonus agreements, and all of the usual major-league restrictions do not apply to our association. There's no obligation on your part, as William's mother, Mrs. Hilton, nor on your son's part. There are no dues, no fees, and no contract to sign. You simply complete an application for membership in our association.

"And as soon as it's signed, you and your son will get a cash bonus! And there's no strings on the money. You keep it. All of it! Even if the association never gets Chip a contract with a major-league organization.

"It's my belief that William, here, will be one of the very select few to realize every boy's dream: playing major league baseball! Our best research estimates that William's signing bonus will be at least *fifty thousand dollars!* And all but 10 percent of that will be yours. You'll get forty-five thousand dollars in addition to the cash bonus you get as soon as you and William sign our association application."

Mary Hilton was just as confused as Chip, but keeping her family going and building a career had given her keen insight into business. "How does the association benefit?" she asked. "How can it afford to do all this?"

"Well, it's privately endowed for one thing," Breen explained, "and its operating expenses are partly covered by the 10 percent of the bonus money an athlete may receive when and if he signs with a big-league organization.

"Then the ten-percent is fed right back into the association to keep the organization going and to help some other worthy athlete. You see, the president of our association is a wealthy baseball fan, and he's interested in kids. He wants to see them get a fair deal. That's why he founded the association. In fact, he endowed it with his personal fortune."

Breen turned to Chip. "Well, young man," he said lightly, "what do you think about our association? Got any questions?"

Chip shook his head. "No," he said uncertainly, "I don't think so. I only want to go to college. That's what I've been planning on."

"That's great!" Breen said briskly. "Won't affect anything. You can go to college and get the money just the same. Furthermore, you'll get a hundred dollars a month all the time you're in college. There's nothing wrong with having extra pizza money, is there?"

Breen nudged the briefcase with his knee and covertly studied their puzzled faces. Then he made his decision.

Rising suddenly, he startled Chip and Mary Hilton by lifting the wide-opened case above his head to send a shower of twenty-dollar bills cascading downward, covering the beige-colored living room rug with a carpet of green.

There was stunned silence. Chip looked at the hundreds of bills in amazement. Mary Hilton's gray eyes were wide with shocked fascination as Hoops jumped and playfully batted the last few spiraling bills floating to the carpet. With a flourish, Breen drew a paper and pen from his pocket and forced them into Chip's hands.

"There you are, son," he said pompously. "There's *your* money! It's *all* yours! *Ten thousand dollars!* Just sign the application and pick up all that cash! It's all yours! There'll be more where that came from, I *assure* you!"

Chip forced his eyes away from the paper he was holding to the pile of bills on the floor. He'd never seen so much money at one time in his life. Ten thousand dollars would pay a huge chunk of college expenses. And if Breen got him a big-league contract, he'd get another bonus which might pay off the mortgage and then his mother could stop working, forever!

He opened the paper and looked searchingly at his mom. Mary Hilton was still astounded by Breen's theatrics! Chip's heart overflowed completely then, love for his mom filling his chest with an almost unbearable pain and choking off his speech completely. He pretended to read the words on the paper, but his eyes were blurred by deep emotion and he couldn't see a thing.

Then Breen made a mistake. He mistook Chip's intense quietness for indecision and pointed to the signature line at the bottom of the page.

"Sign right there, William," he said brusquely. "Remember, you're leaving for Clearview tomorrow. You ought to be in bed. Besides, you've got to talk to your mother about college."

Thirty minutes later Gabby Breen headed back to the Valley Falls Inn. With nervous fingers he tapped the briefcase beside him and shook his head in disbelief. His lips kept forming bitter self-accusations. "Where did I slip up? It always worked before! What went wrong? What's with these people?"

Chip could have answered those questions. Breen's big mistake had been his reference to college. All of Chip's dreams about following in his dad's footsteps and the hopes his mom had so often expressed had flooded his thoughts then, completely drowning out any temptation of money.

Coach Rockwell's words had come rushing back: "An education is an asset that can never dissipate; no one can take it away from you! Money and friends may vanish, but an education sticks forever!"

So Chip had told Breen he wouldn't sign the application until he had talked with his coach. The boy's quiet refusal had startled Breen, and he spent many anxious minutes trying to convince Chip and Mary Hilton how foolish it was to turn down such an opportunity.

"Why, you're sure to get a big-league bonus of fifty thousand dollars—maybe more—and you'll have a salary besides," Breen had argued. "How can you give up all that money? All it takes is your signature."

Chip hadn't said it to Breen, but that was one of the things that had convinced him Breen and his proposition were all wrong. Stu Gardner had warned him that any player who accepted money was a professional, even if he waited until after he graduated from college to play professional ball.

SHORTCUT TO FAME

Breen tried every way he knew to shake the teenager's decision, but Chip had been adamant. In his heart, Breen knew he had lost out, but he kept trying. Gabby finally persuaded Chip to promise to give him a final answer when the Bears played the Raptors in Hedgetown. He then picked up the crisp bills littering the floor and left.

Long after Chip had fallen asleep, Mary Hilton sat thinking about her teenage son and the situations he was now facing and would have to face in later years. She was thankful because Chip had shown he could make his own decisions. Thankful, too, that he hadn't been swept off his feet.

Chip had demonstrated that he was intelligent enough to consider important matters carefully and sensible enough to seek advice from responsible people before rushing impetuously into an important situation. Most of all, she was proud of Chip because he had proved he was strong enough to turn away from a tempting shortcut to fame and fortune.

CHAPTER 8

Pennant Tension

HENRY ROCKWELL leaned back in the tufted, red leather wing chair in his den and stroked the wide arm-rests with both hands as he listened to Chip recount last night's events. His black eyes reflected pleasure when Chip had finished the story, and his words reflected his elation.

"Good! Good for you, Chipper! This guy sounds like a phony. I've never even heard of the Sports Assurance Program. It all sounds fishy to me! No professional base-ball man would ever approach a high school athlete with a proposition like that.

"It actually sounds like this Breen was trying to position himself as your agent. If you had signed that paper, you would have forfeited your *entire* collegiate eligibility in *every* sport. You and your mom did the right thing.

"The fact that this man offered you money to sign with his association, if there even is one, tells me it was a ploy. When you see him in Hedgetown, suggest that he make an appointment with me to talk about his program. Meanwhile, I'll make a few calls. OK? Mark my words, he'll never show up. I'd bet my life on that."

An hour later, with the radio speakers thumping, Biggie, Speed, Red, and Soapy listened to Chip's story as Morris's mostly reliable '65 Mustang drew closer and closer to Clearview. They all completely agreed with Coach Rockwell's conclusion.

Soapy bolted upright in the backseat, "Chip, if you'd signed Breen's paper and then got drafted, he'd have boxed you in! You probably would have ended up playing for whoever drafted you since you couldn't ever play college sports. And everybody knows you want to go to State and play ball like your dad did."

Schwartz declared, "If Rock says this Breen's pulling a fast one, you can bet he's right."

"Stu Gardner warned us about guys like that," Biggie added.

Speed changed the subject. "What about this Scissors Kildane, Chip?" he asked. "Is he really as good as the papers say?"

"Better!" Chip declared. "He's got everything—a fastball, a knuckler, and a curve that looks like it rolls off a table."

"Bears gonna win?" Schwartz queried.

That got Chip started on the Bears, and he was still praising them when the five Valley Falls friends baled out in the parking lot of Clearview's Lion Stadium. It took Chip only a few minutes to get passes for his friends. They headed for the snack bar as Chip headed for the dugout.

Corky Squill had been watching the players' gate all through the warm-up. When Chip came out on the field and headed for the dugout, Corky casually sauntered over for a drink of water. "Hi ya, Chip," he smiled. "Glad you're back. We missed you."

Scissors Kildane came striding up in time to hear Corky's words. "That's right, kid," he said. "We missed you throwing batting practice. Eddie wants you to throw again today if your arm's OK."

Squill hung around, eager to quiz Chip to find out if Breen had sealed the deal. He was thinking about the three thousand dollars he'd mentally been spending. When Kildane rejoined the pitchers, Corky sidled closer to Chip and lowered his voice.

"Breen drive you up?" he asked quietly.

Chip shook his head. "No. I came up with my friends."

"He took you home, didn't he?"

"Oh, sure, but then he went on to Hedgetown. Or at least that's where he said he was going."

"He talk to your folks?"

Chip was surprised by the peppering of questions. "Yes," he said thoughtfully. "Mr. Breen talked to my mom."

Squill waited expectantly, his quick, black eyes suddenly sharp and penetrating.

"And?" he said, waiting for more.

"That's about all."

Eddie Duer saved Chip then, sending the Bears out on the field for batting practice.

Squill was disappointed. He hadn't learned anything. Maybe the kid had a deal with the Drakes all along. Gabby had been worried about Stu Gardner and his friendliness with Duer. Corky glanced sourly at Duer. "Maybe Eddie's in on it too," he muttered. "I wouldn't put it past him."

Duer named Phil Akers to start for the Bears. The tall 220-pounder had been used most of the season as a relief pitcher. Kildane's much needed rest had forced Duer to put Akers into the starting rotation. Phil was fast but wild, and his erratic throwing kept the Bears in hot water all afternoon.

The Lions, fighting desperately to hold their spot at the top of the second division and taking full advantage of Akers's wildness, got out in front 2-0 in the first, and didn't need their half of the ninth, winning comfortably, 8-3.

Chip took the defeat as hard as the Bears players. He had wanted his Valley Falls friends to see the league leaders at their best. Corky Squill had been the biggest disappointment. The stocky second baseman had a miserable day in the field, booting three chances and going none for four at bat.

The strength of any baseball team is down the middle—from the catcher to the pitcher, the second baseman, and the center fielder. That line of strength was weakened by Akers's wildness and Squill's errors, and that made the difference.

After the game, Chip and his Valley Falls friends joined Kildane for burgers and a movie. Angry with himself for his bad day, Corky Squill sulked in sullen silence in his room and waited impatiently for Gabby Breen's call.

As the hours wore on, Squill's anxiety increased and he paced the floor. When the call came at nine o'clock, Squill pounced on the bed and had the receiver to his ear before the first ring ended. But he got little information. Gabby Breen was a careful man. He wasn't going to hold a lengthy conversation over the phone, and Squill agreed to meet him.

Corky Squill was cautious too. He wasn't going to take any chances with the league's fraternizing rule.

DUGOUT JINX

Eddie Duer was a stickler for league rules and demanded his players follow them to the letter. Duer wouldn't even permit his Bears players to talk to players of other clubs off the field. "You can nod to 'em," he would warn, "but that's all. No conversations and no friendship stuff! You pal up with your own teammates!"

Corky got out of the taxi and walked the last two blocks to Breen's motel. Making sure he was still unobserved, Squill knocked on the door. Inside, without a word of greeting, he plunged right in.

"What happened?" Squill demanded. "I couldn't get a thing out of Hilton."

Breen's face flushed red. "Me neither," he admitted sourly. "Gardner must've gotten to him. The kid claims he isn't interested in being drafted. Says he's gonna do just what his dad did. Tried to feed me a lot of nonsense about ethics and professionalism."

"What about the money? How about the briefcase?"

"Didn't work. Their stupid cat was the only one to touch the bills. Something's wrong though. Father's dead, mother has to work, and they've got a mortgage on the house. I—I can't figure it out."

"The kid's clever," Squill mused. "I bet he's counting on a deal with the Drakes."

Breen shrugged his shoulders and flattened his hands in a gesture of disgust. "Forget it," he said bitterly. "We've got other things to think about. Guess you know the Lions took two from us, and that means Boots is gonna be history.

"I'm going to Hedgetown early in the morning. If the Panthers take us tomorrow, it'd be smart for me to be around when Kearns cans Rines. Now listen. If that happens, I'll be in charge of the Raptors for the Bears game

Saturday afternoon sure as anything, and that's why we gotta get together. Right?"

"I guess so," Squill said reluctantly, "but I don't see where I come in."

"You come in as my field captain next year, that's where you come in! But I can't wait until next year to sell you to Kearns. I wanna sell him on you right now, the very first day I'm in charge of the Raptors. Get it?"

Squill nodded dubiously. Breen was too quick for Corky, too crafty.

"You see," Breen continued, "the minute Kearns appoints me manager I'm gonna start talkin' about next year, and I'm gonna tell him you're the guy we need to give us the pennant. But, like I said before, I gotta sell Kearns on the idea that you're a hustler, a fighter, and a real leader. That means you gotta go back to your old style in the field. Think of it, you'll get a big jump in salary and be the captain of the Raptors—and you'll be workin' with me."

Squill was visibly impressed. This was the out he had wanted, the chance he had dreamed about. He hated Eddie Duer because the manager made him toe the mark on and off the field. His thoughts went winging into the future.

"But you're the one who changed my style of play," Squill replied, puzzled. "You told me to change. You never told me why, but you said I moved around too much. I don't get it!"

Breen's lips tightened in a mirthless grin. "You don't have to get it. You just do as I say! Start it in the Bears practice tomorrow. All I want you to do is go back to the original style.

"Now listen! You guys will get to Hedgetown about nine o'clock," Breen said glibly. "You can reach me at this number. Call me just as soon as you get in town. If the Raptors lose tomorrow, kid, I'll have some good news for both of us, and you'll be on your way."

Eddie Duer faced the danger of a league-leading team becoming overconfident. Now that the Bears had lost two straight games to second-division teams, he was all the more determined to insist on the off-day practice. Chip and Scissors were among the first to be dressed and out on the field. Duer was talking to Mickey Curry and greeted them with a quick smile.

"No throwing for you today, Chip," Duer said. "Every other day will be enough. Today you chase some flies, take a turn at bat, and generally take it easy. How's that front office work?"

Chip smiled. "Just finished my time in the publicity department, and they let me write a press release. I don't think they'll use it, but I like to write. This is what I like best though—being on the field with the team!"

"What some managers won't do to impress a youngster," Scissors wisecracked.

"You mean till they get 'em drafted," Curry quipped. "The guy never gives me any rest."

On his way to the outfield, Chip trotted past Corky Squill. "Hi ya, Corky. I'm backing you up."

Squill deliberately turned his back and pretended he had not heard Chip. The slight was obvious, and Chip was perplexed.

Corky was irked. He was certain Chip had lied to Breen about college and being uninterested in the draft. Bitterness filled his heart, and his resentment toward Chip grew as he thought about the three thousand dollars he'd lost.

Eddie Duer added fuel to the flames of Corky's anger when he brought up Squill's sloppy play from the previous day. Duer didn't stop there. The aggressive manager went right down the line, giving each player a dressing down. Then he concentrated on the infielders, drilling them again and again on double-play combinations and plays to the plate.

The entire pitching staff chased flies in the outfield. Kildane, Richards, Mills, Akers, Burns, Goodman, and Falls were hustling as much as the outfielders. Chip took his turn, too, thrilled by the opportunity to pull in a long fly from the bat of Ketch Kerrigan. Kerrigan was the strongest man on the squad and could hit the ball a mile. Duer often used him as a clutch pinch hitter, and the big man invariably came through.

After a full hour of fielding, Duer was satisfied and gathered the squad at home plate, but he wasn't through. The skillful manager realized his young club had reached the crucial point of the campaign, the point where pennant tension had begun to tell. This team could lose its poise and its effectiveness overnight. The coming two-game series with the Raptors probably would tell the story. Duer's pleased expression masked the keen appraisal he made of each player as he talked.

"We've been sloppy on the bases, and we've slipped up on a couple of signs when it hurt. Slapping fines on a player who misses a sign doesn't help anyone, and I've tried to avoid it. But there's no excuse for missing a sign when all you have to do is step out of the box or call for a repeat if you're on base.

"So we'll spend the next half hour reviewing the signs. Let me have the regular batting order. Pitchers, cover the bases. Chip, you used to work behind the mask; suppose you handle the plate."

"I wanna play first!" Kildane chortled. "Come on, guys. We'll show 'em some classy fielding!"

DUGOUT JINX

Windy Mills winked at Sid Goodman as the two left-ies wheeled around and dashed for shortstop and second base. Dante Burns trotted down to the hot corner. Richards, Akers, and Falls headed for the outfield. Chip started the ball around the horn and, after it made the rounds, tossed it to Duer. For thirty minutes the hard-working manager called the situations, gave the signs, and then fungoed the ball while the regulars ran the plays. Not a sign was missed.

"Nice work! You guys are a real team!" Duer said, calling them to the plate once more. "Let's have a couple of sprints and finish up with some hitting. First, we'll take the infielders. Line up at the grandstand and finish at second base.

"Bob, you start 'em, and I'll clock the winners. Chip, you can go with the pitchers."

Corky Squill, by far the fastest infielder on the team, won easily. Surprising enough, Stretch Johnson came in second. The tall first baseman took tremendous strides but couldn't overcome Squill's fast start. Bill Dawson, the speedy left fielder, nipped Norm Klein in the outfielder's race, and Chip led the pitchers all the way, winning by five yards. Windy Mills and Scissors Kildane matched stride for stride until the very end when Mills forged ahead.

"All right," Duer shouted. "All first- and second-place winners. A new glove for the winner. Line 'em up, Bob."

"Hilton'll win," Kildane shouted, "or dinner's on me! Any takers?"

"Against the field?" Whitey Falls demanded.

"Sure!"

"It's a deal!"

"You're making a mistake, Scissors," Chip protested. "You'd better not."

"I already have," Kildane retorted.

"OK, guys, let's go," Bob Reiter said briskly. "Line up as I call your names. Johnson, Klein, Dawson, Mills, Hilton, and Squill. Don't go until I reach the count of three. Got it? OK. On your mark! Get set! One-two-three!"

Corky Squill was the only runner who tried to beat the count, breaking on Reiter's "two!" The split-second advantage shot him three strides ahead. Chip broke out a little late, but when he sped past the plate, he was only a yard behind Corky. Chip could tell from the yelling that the race was between him and Squill, and he really began to pump his arms.

"Come on, Chip, you've got him," Kildane roared.

Halfway to the pitcher's mound, Chip pulled even with the speeding infielder and forged ahead. Then before he could lengthen out his long legs, he felt a vicious jab in the ribs and almost fell. As he tried to regain his stride, he heard Squill's mocking laugh and saw the fleet infielder spurt out in front.

Even as he stumbled, Chip could hardly believe it, that Corky would do that. But it was true, and Chip knew it. Corky Squill had elbowed him intentionally. Chip tried to figure out the reason as he dug his spikes desperately into the turf.

"Foul!" Kildane shouted. "Foul!"

Chip wasn't finished. He'd been put through the wringer in broken-field running with a football under his arm and had mastered the knack of regaining his balance quickly. Now he churned his feet until he was almost upright and then dug after Klein, who had edged ahead and was now second to Squill.

Corky thought he had the race won, so he let up a little and made the mistake of looking back. He couldn't believe his eyes! Chip had regained his stride, had passed Klein, and was only a yard behind. Almost before Corky could whip his head back around, Chip was alongside him. The two straining figures held even for a second, but only for a second as Chip's long strides ate up the distance and drew him steadily ahead. He held his pace to cross the finish line a full yard ahead of Squill.

Chip heard Kildane's triumphant shout as he eased off and slowed down to a slow trot. Then someone grabbed him by the arm and spun him around. It was Squill, his features distorted with rage.

"What's the idea of elbowin' me?" Corky demanded. "Is that the kind of guy you are?"

Chip stared at Squill in astonishment. He was caught by surprise, left speechless. "I never elbowed you, Corky—"

Squill flung Chip's arm roughly aside. "Don't give me that!"

Scissors Kildane came running up, his pleasant features unusually serious. "I saw it, Corky," he said quietly. "You did the elbowing. You owe Chip an apology."

Squill's face purpled. "Me apologize?" he yelled. "Me apologize to that cheat? Forget it! Forget you too, man!"

"That's enough, Corky," Eddie Duer said harshly. "We saw it, so drop it! Chip won and you lost, and that's all there is to it. All right, everyone, that's all!"

But it wasn't all and everybody on the field knew it. Corky Squill was a hard loser, and the incident wasn't over by any means. Chip Hilton had brought out the wrath of the bitter infielder, and that could mean trouble—for the young intern, for Scissors Kildane, and perhaps for the whole club. It might even mean the pennant.

CHAPTER 9

An Outsider and a Jinx

HUNTER KEARNS was in a foul mood. The current Raptors losing streak had just about knocked his team out of the pennant race, and the Hedgetown fans were blaming Boots Rines. Kearns liked the tall, easygoing manager and had stuck by him through all the weeks of criticism. But baseball had become a business. The financially strapped real estate developer and Raptor owner couldn't afford sentiment and wouldn't take the writers' and fans' harassment.

Baseball fans pay the salaries of players and managers, and the Hedgetown rooters had begun to use the weapon that hurts most—the empty seat. The Hedgetown fans had practically deserted the same team that had won the championship a short year before. Kearns knew a drastic change was imperative. He glanced up impatiently.

"Been expecting you. I felt foolish calling the head office again just before the draft telling them to forget about this Hilton kid after your assurances. What happened?"

"Just couldn't sign that kid no way," Breen replied. "Here's your money back," he added, as he handed Kearns a cashier's check from the Valley Falls National Bank.

Kearns motioned to a chair beside the desk. "Sit down, Gabby. Tell me again."

"Well, just like I told you over the phone, I drove him home and sounded him out and figured he'd go with me. Anyway, I pulled out all the stops and thought I had him. But he stuck to the college idea. I figure Gardner already got to the kid."

Kearns shook his head. "No, Gabby, you're wrong. I've known Stu Gardner for a long time. He plays it straight. No team drafted Hilton. Seems they knew he was set on school and took him at his word and didn't risk a pick—like we almost did."

"Could be," Breen said reluctantly.

Kearns's voice had a slight edge when he continued. "Never mind that, Gabby. There's more important work to be done right now. Guess you've seen the papers. Seems like everybody in town is down on Rines. They even blame him when the Bears beat other teams. If we lose today, we're practically out of the race. I'll have to make some sort of a move, or that park will be empty the rest of the season. You prepared to take over if a change has to be made?"

Breen didn't answer immediately. He wanted to give the appearance of weighing the proposition carefully and reluctantly. "I guess I'm prepared, Mr. Kearns," he said thoughtfully. "Of course I don't feel too good about Boots, but I guess someone has to take over, and if you want me—"

"I wouldn't ask you if I didn't," Kearns said shortly. "Suppose we leave it this way: if the Panthers beat us this afternoon, Boots is out and you're in."

Breen nodded, and it was all he could do to mask the exultation flooding his eyes. One thing was for sure: The Panthers' number one fan this afternoon would be Gabby Breen!

Kearns swung around in his chair. "Might as well sit with me and listen to the game," he said with a half-smile. "First time I ever let the results of a single game influence my selection of a manager."

During the next hour and thirty minutes, Gabby Breen gave Hunter Kearns a command performance of his acting ability. He moaned and groaned through every inning as the Panthers heaped it on the faltering Raptors.

Hunter Kearns gave up in the sixth inning when the Panthers went out in front 11-2. As he slumped in his office chair, he debated his managerial crisis. At any rate, the dropping of Boots Rines would appease the wolves until the end of this season.

He began to reevaluate Breen, wondering if he wasn't making a mistake. But he knew the flashy scout was popular with the fans and writers, and he hoped the man might be the catalyst—even an interim one—to pull the team out of their slump.

When the last Raptors hitter struck out in the top of the ninth, Kearns stretched out his hand and grasped the hand of his new manager.

"You take charge first thing in the morning, Gabby," he said decisively. "We've lost three straight, so it isn't a bad spot for you. The law of averages ought to start working, and maybe you'll get off on the right foot. I guess I don't have to tell you how much these two home games with the Bears mean. If we can win both, we'll still be in the race. Well, good luck! You'll need it!"

Breen's heart was thumping with excitement. "Thanks, Mr. Kearns," he managed. "Don't worry about these two games. We're gonna take 'em both! I know what I'm talkin' about!"

"I sure hope so," Kearns said ruefully. "Oh, by the way, keep quiet about Boots. I want to let him know about the change first, before I release it to the papers. I hate to feed Boots to the wolves, but it's the only out I have. Meet me here tomorrow morning at nine o'clock. I'll call a meeting for ten o'clock and turn the team over to you at that time.

"You'd better be lining up your pitching plans. Murph will help you. He knows exactly how we stack up as of this minute. Turner worked today, and Baker pitched Wednesday. That means that anyone else you want to use tomorrow ought to be OK. See you in the morning."

Breen's mind was working feverishly. Now to see Corky. It was a good thing he'd told Squill to call him tonight.

Kate Dobson, Kearns's secretary, never glanced up when Breen left the office but kept her brown eyes focused on her computer screen. When Kearns called her, she walked just a little too briskly into the inner office, her leather heels clicking defiantly on the hardwood floor.

Kearns knew his secretary was displeased, and he also knew why. Nonetheless he gave no sign, spoke in a soft voice, and asked her to have the club attorney draw up a new contract for Nelson Breen, who would manage the Raptors for the remainder of the season.

Miss Dobson bore down so heavily on her notepad that the pencil snapped. "Darn," she said in disgust. "Nothing seems to be going right around here!"

Kearns grinned slightly. "Having trouble?" he asked.

"Not half the trouble you're going to have with your new manager," she said, walking briskly from the office.

Kearns pondered Miss Dobson's words. He had experienced the same foreboding every time he'd considered Breen for Rines's job. He shook his head. Kate Dobson was a good reader of people, and it was fairly obvious she'd given Nelson "Gabby" Breen an extremely low rating. Kearns sighed. It was too late now; it was done. He'd just have to hope for the best.

Meanwhile, the Bears were on the team bus traveling to Hedgetown. The two defeats and the previous afternoon's incident had created tension within the squad. Despite the atmosphere, Eddie Duer sat beside Chip most of the trip and talked to him about his pitching. The husky manager was fond of Chip. Duer liked the boy's work ethic as well as his keen interest in baseball. The bus ride gave them their first real opportunity to talk baseball.

"Chip," Duer said pleasantly, "you're with us because you were the tournament MVP and you really love baseball. Stu Gardner happens to be one of my best friends, and he told me all about your plans for college. I'm all for that!

"While you're with us," Duer continued, "we want to help you with your pitching. So if you have no objections, one of us will talk to you every day. I'm taking the lead because I'm the top man.

"First, let's start with your delivery. Guess you won't mind a few constructive comments, especially when they're for your own good. For one thing, you don't conceal the ball. The more you can hide the ball from the hitters, the less chance they have to focus on it and get set.

"Some pitchers show the ball to the batter several times and then hide it at the last moment. Others never show the ball to the hitter, keeping it hidden in their gloves and behind their legs and bodies until it seems to come out of nowhere. Some let you see the ball when they start their deliveries and then hide it until it suddenly pops over the plate.

"You've got to decide on a certain kind of delivery and then stick to it. Another thing, you've got to learn to use the same delivery for every pitch. Every pitch must look alike as far as your delivery is concerned. Get it? Good! Now, I'll let Curry have you."

Duer stood up in the aisle and called to the burly catcher. "Hey, Mickey! Talk to Hilton!"

Curry swung around in his seat and nodded his head. "Sure," he boomed. "I wanna tell him how to keep runners from gettin' too big of a lead." He looked significantly at Windy Mills as he lumbered down the aisle.

Mills grunted. "Hah! Catchers with washed-up arms always blame the pitchers."

"Some pitchers I know ought to go back to high school and get a little coaching," the popular captain murmured.

Curry seemed to overflow into the aisle and against Chip when he sat down. The big catcher's arm was the talk of the league. The ball was just a flash of light between the plate and the bases when he tried to catch a runner, and there wasn't a Bears infielder who didn't complain about the heavy ball the burly receiver threw. He nudged Chip with his hard right arm.

"You've got a lot of stuff, kid, a lot of stuff. A year with us and you'd be ready for the big show. I don't know what Eddie Duer told you, but I'll just talk about pitchin' in general and maybe you'll get something out of it.

"There're all kinds of pitchers, Chip. Some are temperamental, some are mean, and some are pleasant and easygoin' like Scissors. You're a lot like Scissors. You've both got a lot of speed and a slider and a change-up, and you've both got control. What's more important, you're hard workers and team players.

"Kildane's the answer to a manager's prayer, Chip. You know why? He's one of those rubber-arm guys who wants to do all the pitching. If he had his way, he'd pitch every day. You know, he'd be priceless in the majors as a fireman. Eddie uses him like that now, and that's why this bunch of kids is winning. We all know Kildane's the difference. We'd be just another young ball club—except for me, of course—if it weren't for Scissors. Most hurlers have to have their rest—but not Scissors! All he needs is a yawn, and he's ready!

"Today's baseball is power-hitting baseball, and every manager in the game is looking for guys who can smack it out of the park. But every manager knows you must have top pitching and a reliable relief man or two in the bullpen if you're going to be leading the pack in September.

"That's why Scissors has meant so much to us. Every time one of the other guys gets in a jam, Scissors is on Eddie to put him in so he can put out the fire. Maybe I'm talking too much about the big beanpole, but all I can say is he's one of the best. If you pattern yourself after Scissors Kildane, you'll be headin' in the right direction."

Curry talked to Chip all the way into Hedgetown, but the rest of the players were unusually quiet. Most of the Bears were trying to catch up on their sleep—all except Corky Squill. He was sitting in the rear of the bus, sulking and thinking about Chip Hilton and Eddie Duer. At that moment, he hated one just about as much as the other.

DUGOUT JINX

Corky Squill was the sort of player his nickname implied. He seemed always to bob up at the right time and in the right place. But he hadn't always been like that. In fact, Squill probably would have fallen away from baseball if it hadn't been for Gabby Breen.

Several years earlier, when Squill was eighteen, Gabby Breen had signed Corky to a contract. Gabby didn't believe Squill was going anywhere, but he'd signed him anyway.

The next spring, Breen was asked to assemble a new team for an industrial league that was operating on a shoestring budget. Squill had joined the squad.

Breen stuck around long enough to get the shoestring and the team. It wasn't much of an outfit, but it was good enough to beat the local competition. To pass the time, Gabby really coached. He held daily practices and strategy sessions at night. The league folded after a month, but during that month Gabby had seriously worked with the only potential ballplayer on the team—Corky Squill.

Corky had one serious fault as an infielder that, if not corrected, would keep him from ever getting anywhere in professional baseball: he telegraphed the catcher's signals by his very actions on the diamond. The batter only had to watch the excitable second baseman to know what kind of pitch was next. Breen gave himself the task of breaking the exuberant Corky of his playing habits at second base.

Gabby Breen was Corky's hero, and he set out to be a miniature Breen, mimicking everything the flashy manager did—his speech, his dress, and his actions. It wasn't surprising that he followed Breen's orders to the letter.

Gabby changed Corky's style of play and toned down his cocky behavior so much that Corky became just the opposite of his former self. In the beginning, Squill had captured the attention of the local fans because of his crowd-pleasing attributes, and Gabby Breen couldn't stand that kind of competition. Gabby had to be the center of attention when it came to showmanship. So he'd stepped on Corky, squelching his energy and his extravagant gestures in the field and at bat.

Almost overnight, it seemed, Corky Squill developed into a closemouthed, silent player who concentrated solely upon fielding, throwing, and hitting. He steeled himself to such an extent that he became robotic in the field, silent and motionless until the ball came his way. His actions never again betrayed a pitch or a play.

Corky had continued to play that way because Gabby Breen had said that was the type of ballplayer he should become if he wanted to make good. This on-the-field behavior had carried over into his general personality until he became morose and moody. His Bears teammates had tried to loosen him up but had found him impossible. Now they accepted him as he preferred to be, silent and efficient, a loner.

Squill was glad when the bus rolled into Hedgetown. He wanted to find out how Breen had made out with the managing job, and he was disgusted with all the attention Chip Hilton was receiving. But, silent as he'd been on the bus, he couldn't resist a contemptuous jab in Duer's direction when they unloaded in front of the hotel.

"Two in a row to the two weakest teams in the league," Corky said bitterly. "What is this? Little League? We gonna throw away the pennant just to help some high school nobody?"

Eddie Duer wheeled around and grabbed Squill by the arm. "Enough, Corky," he said coolly. "We didn't lose those two games because of the tournament."

"How about the bench rule?" Corky demanded belligerently. "How about an outsider in the dugout? Every player knows an outsider in the dugout is a jinx!"

"That remark just cost you fifty dollars," Duer said grimly. "See me in my room at eight o'clock. Understand?"

Squill contemptuously shrugged his shoulders and turned away. There was an awkward silence as the other players ignored the incident and busied themselves unloading their bags.

Chip was humiliated. His face reddened as he tried his best to pretend he hadn't heard Squill's remarks, but every word had burned itself into his heart. He lugged his bag into the lobby and sank down into a chair. So that was it! Corky Squill thought Chip Hilton was an outsider and a jinx.

CHAPTER 10

Ice Water in His Veins

EDDIE DUER had been in baseball a long time—first as a minor-league player, later as a scrappy infielder in the majors, then back to the minors, and finally as a successful manager for the Drake organization. Duer had been a tremendous success with the Parkville club. The fans liked him, and Duer had the complete confidence of the owners. Duer realized the multiple objectives of his job. He was responsible for developing young players and for fielding a winning team.

Duer proved a team could be popular as long as it was a hustling club and played heads-up ball. Eddie had earned his success, working hard with his young players and at the job of pleasing the fans. His success had never gone to his head, and he became more than a successful baseball manager in the eyes of the Parkville citizens— he became one of them, one of their own.

Duer was right at home in his job and in Parkville, and he was proud of his team. After all, they were chiefly kids. Now, as he sat in his room waiting for Corky Squill, he was thinking about the young players, the rookies, who'd made such a gallant showing. He thought about each one, right through the batting order.

Corky Squill, the leadoff hitter, had what it takes to be a real ballplayer, if you could separate him from his surly disposition. He was fast, had a good arm, and played to win. He was usually ahead of the play in his mind and seldom failed to make the right move. As a leadoff man he was ideal, worked the pitcher into a hole more often than not, got on base one way or another, and was smart and fast on the base paths. Furthermore, he hit a consistent .300. But he was antagonistic and temperamental, a victim to the traits that had spoiled the careers of hundreds of big-league prospects.

"Why can't he be like Damon?" Duer murmured. "What in the world's wrong with the guy?"

Damon Boyd, the other member of the keystone double-play combination, was exactly the opposite of Corky Squill. Damon was the spark of the team, a hustler in every situation, and as friendly as they come. He was a master of the drag bunt and as fast as a streak.

The number three hitter, Bill Dawson, covered left field like a blanket, had a good arm, was fast, and hit a solid .290 from the first-base side of the plate.

"Bill's going places," Duer muttered. "Nice kid!"

The cleanup spot was filled by Stretch Johnson. The big batter hit and threw left-handed, and he was considered the best first baseman in the league.

"In his second year too," Duer said enthusiastically, nodding toward the empty chair facing him, remembering the big, gangly kid who'd tripped over every blade of grass in Bear Stadium's outfield until he'd worked the kid out at first base. Duer chuckled. "Even fooled me, the way he came along."

The smile was still hovering on Duer's lips as he thought of his other regulars. Shifting to the outfield for his fifth and sixth hitters, he thought about Norm Klein and Ted Smith. Klein was one of those big players who seemed to smell a hit coming before the batter tagged the ball, and he made the catch look easy. He hit a long ball and was a hit with every fan and teammate because of his hustle and friendliness.

Smith was a rookie, playing his first professional baseball, but he played right field like a veteran. The tall novice could make the long throws and was hitting like a fiend.

"Over his head, maybe," Duer solemnly assured the chair, "but he's bound to be called up next year or the year after."

Duer's eyes glistened when he thought of his seventh hitter. Hale was everyone's favorite. The third baseman looked like a high school freshman with his blond, short-cropped hair and his scrubbed face, but he didn't handle the hot corner like a freshman. The kid threw the ball on a string, and his glove ate up everything that came his way.

"Isn't bad with the bat, either," Duer confided to the chair. "All I need is one more year with him, and he'll be ready. Gotta give Mickey a lot of credit though. He was right when he said Pauly belonged on third."

That brought Duer to Mickey Curry, the workhorse catcher of the Bears. The burly field captain worked behind the plate day after day, and it was Mickey's leadership almost as much as his own, Duer thought happily, that held the team together. He'd have been lost without Mickey.

Duer leaned forward, his words barely audible. "You know," he whispered, "Mickey's the best thing that ever happened to me and Parkville. He's *made* baseball in this town." Duer leaned back in his chair, thinking about his best friend.

Mickey Curry could have gone up to the Drakes a dozen times, but he wouldn't leave Duer and Parkville. "Me," the human bulldozer would growl pleasantly, "I'm a small-town player. I like the sticks. Besides, the Drakes already got a couple of catchers, and I like to play every day."

Duer relaxed comfortably in his chair and began thinking about his pitching staff. Unfortunately these thoughts weren't so good, and little by little he straightened up. Kildane was overworked, tight as a drum, and badly in need of a rest. If they could only get by these next two games with the Raptors, he could rest Scissors and get him ready for the key games down the stretch. But who could he use now?

The last two games had been disastrous. Richards had come down with a bad arm in the second game with the Hornets, and Akers's erratic pitching at Clearview yesterday had given the Lions the 8-3 victory. Forgetting Whitey Falls and Sid Goodman, who were nursing bad arms, that left Windy Mills and Dante Burns, and the Raptors "owned" them both.

"It all adds up to Scissors," he said bitterly, "just as it has all year. Maybe I could try Troy tomorrow? . . . No, he's almost as overworked as Scissors, and the Raptors love his soft stuff. I'd better hold him for Sun—"

Duer's one-way conversation was interrupted by Corky's knock on the door. Squill had heard the murmur of Duer's words and was surprised to find the manager alone.

"Sit down, Corky," Duer said pleasantly. "You guys have got me talking to myself."

Duer studied Squill's sullen face as the moody second baseman sat down. Then the manager's gentle and persuasive voice continued, "You were off base this afternoon, Corky, way off. I hated to hand you that fine, but you left me no choice. What's bothering you?"

"Plenty!" Squill said sharply, his black eyes glittering angrily. "What is this, a ball club or a baseball clinic for high school hotshots?"

Duer's placid features tightened and his jaw line bulged. Not all the strain in a tight baseball race is borne by the players. The manager's burden is a heavy one, and every decision down the stretch becomes momentous. Eddie Duer was a fighter—quick, intent, and sure of himself. Although he was an extremely friendly person, pennant tension was beginning to take a toll on everyone.

Squill's contemptuous attitude and biting words now struck fire with Duer and sent a burst of rage rushing through his whole body. It required every ounce of self-control to restrain the angry words on his tongue, but he forced them back and spoke calmly.

"Corky, the Bears are a good baseball club. Your job is to play ball the best you know how and to follow the instructions of the manager. My job is to run the ball club and cooperate with the management. It seems to me you're forgetting that your job has nothing to do with general policies or with managing the club."

"What about the playing field? On the field?"

"I don't quite understand what you're getting at. As a player, your job is chiefly concerned with playing ball."

"And how about the dugout?" Corky challenged.

"You have your player rights there too."

"Well, as a player tryin' to win the pennant, haven't I got any right to complain when you let a kid jinx this club by sittin' down on the bench, smirkin' and actin' like a big deal—"

Duer rose to his feet. The muscles of his face were contracted, and his complexion was fiery red although his voice remained calm. "That's enough, Corky. Before you came up here, I'd hoped we could handle this on a friendly basis—forget the fine and start all over. But you're impossible!

"So get this! Play your position and keep your mouth shut—about the high school tournament and about strangers on the bench and about Chip Hilton—or Bud Cooke takes over at second and stays there whether we win the pennant or not! Got it? Furthermore, this afternoon's fine stands, plus I'm slapping another one on you for tonight's insubordination! Good night!"

Corky Squill backed out of Duer's room, but he was fuming as he went slowly down the hall. He was filled with hatred for Eddie Duer and the kid he blamed for all his trouble, Chip Hilton. Not only was he out three thousand, now he was out a hundred dollars thanks to Chip Hilton!

Squill left the hotel and hurried along the streets until he found a phone. His furious mind tried to devise some way to get even with his two enemies. He'd call Gabby. At least Gabby was the kind of man he could talk to. Maybe it was fraternizing, but the heck with it! Anyway, he wanted to know how Gabby was making out with the manager's job. Duer couldn't do any more than he was doing already . . . taking his pay . . . and threatening to replace him. Hah! Everyone knew Cooke couldn't even carry his spikes!

Duer was stubborn, especially when he was angry. Corky wondered if maybe he'd better just play it smart and play ball for now and wait for a chance to get even. He might spoil his whole career if Duer benched him now. The best thing he could do was to play ball the way Gabby wanted him to play and hope Hunter Kearns would be impressed. Still it was gonna be tough acting enthusiastic when he didn't feel it.

While Corky Squill was cooling off, Gabby Breen was pacing his room, impatiently waiting for Squill's call. Corky was vital in Breen's plans, and he was worried the volatile second baseman might not call him.

Finally, at 9:30, the phone rang. It was Squill.

"We're in, Corky!" Breen shouted gleefully. "I've got the job! Start in the morning! How's that for good news?"

Squill was doubtful. "Funny," he said uncertainly, "we got in before dinner and no one said anything about it."

"No one knows about it," Breen said exuberantly. "Come on over! Hurry! We're on our way to big times, kid!"

Chip joined Kildane at the breakfast table the next morning and right away he sensed something was up. He glanced around quickly. All the players were talking animatedly. Kildane shoved a newspaper toward him.

"Read the headline, Chip," he said pointedly.

Chip glanced down and almost jumped. He understood what had caused the interest now. Then he turned back to the story.

Boots Rines Resigns as Manager of Raptors
Gabby Breen Takes Charge Today

Hunter Kearns announced exclusively to the *Courier* last night that Steve "Boots" Rines has submitted his resignation as manager of the Hedgetown Raptors, effective immediately. Kearns stated the resignation had been accepted and that Nelson "Gabby" Breen, the popular Raptors scout, would assume charge beginning with today's game against the Bears. It has been evident for some time that a change was imperative, and the *Courier* wishes to assure the fans this paper strongly supports the change.

Breen in Tight Spot

The new manager, Gabby Breen, takes charge of a team that, on paper, is the strongest in the Midwestern League. Yet the Raptors have trailed the Parkville Bears all season, showing no evidence of the fire and effectiveness that carried them to the pennant last year. Losses during the two-day series, which opens here this afternoon, would be disastrous, since the Bears lead by five games in the win column and the Raptors have dropped four more in the all-important loss column. Breen was not immediately available for comment, but the *Courier* joins Hedgetown's fans in wishing the new manager good luck.

"What do you think of that?" Kildane demanded.

Chip shook his head. "I don't know," he said slowly. "I didn't get to know Mr. Breen very well."

"Just as well," Kildane said shortly. "He's bad news! Can't understand why they'd choose him over Rines, but it's none of my business. I know one thing for sure—we can look for some interesting tactics now."

"You mean heckling?"

"Right. Trouble on the field too! At least Breen's got that kind of reputation. Well, we'll see."

Kildane saw, all right, and so did Chip. Breen started what he called his "aggressive baseball strategy" with the first pitch that Red Willis, the Raptors' big left-hander, threw to Damon Boyd.

Squill had flied out deep to right field, and when Damon strolled up to the plate, it seemed like an invitation for the Raptors to start what was to be an exciting afternoon. Catcalls, whistles, and then a pitch that headed straight for Boyd's head—which the short-stop evaded only by an eyelash—were just the beginning.

Chip felt sure Willis had thrown an intentional duster. As the game continued, Chip had no reason to change his mind. Willis's apparent wildness was effective; the Bears went down one, two, three.

During the warm-up, Scissors had tried to inveigle Duer into letting him pitch. Although Kildane used every argument he could think of, the manager had made up his mind to go with Windy Mills. That was a mistake.

The big left-hander was strong and fast enough, but he had no control. The Raptors had his number—not so much because they could hit against him, but because they could upset him. A little heckling from the Raptors dugout went a long way with Mills. Boots Rines had controlled it to a certain extent, but there was no control today. It was Gabby Breen himself who took the lead, and that was all the Raptors and the Hedgetown fans needed.

Mills's unsteadiness seemed to spread to the whole club. Corky even seemed jittery; at least Chip thought so. For the first time since he'd seen Squill play, the second baseman seemed full of pep. He was on the move constantly, immediately after the signs and before and after each pitch. He'd suddenly become a bundle of energy, yelling and pepping it up to everyone's surprise.

Chip couldn't understand the sudden change in Corky. Scissors had said that Corky had ice water in his veins. Well, it must have come to a sudden boil! The Bears' keystone guardian acted as though he'd run into a hornet's nest. Chip concentrated on the Bears second baseman. Something had happened to the Corky Squill he'd come to know.

CHAPTER 11

A Melee and a Massacre

SCISSORS KILDANE was the toast of the Midwestern League, but he was still just a youngster, what you might call a second-year rookie. Most fans forgot that the tall, poised pitcher who'd carved out a record of 12-4 in his rookie year and who'd already won 13 in his sophomore year of professional baseball was barely twenty-one years old. His natural coordination and pitching savvy on the diamond gave the impression that he was an experienced veteran. However, under the Bears cap and uniform, Scissors Kildane was a humble, friendly, overgrown kid with a lot of the old college try and spirit who had proved he was no sophomore flop. That was why he agonized every time a hit rang off the Raptors' bats.

Kildane was with Windy Mills on every pitch. From the bullpen his eyes kept shifting from the mound to the dugout, searching for Eddie Duer and wondering why the peppery little manager didn't call him to come in and put out the fire.

The Raptors went out in front 3-0 before the Bears could retire the side. At that, it needed a sparkling double play—Boyd to Squill to Johnson with three aboard—to save Mills from an avalanche.

The top of the second brought up the Bears's long-ball hitters—Johnson, Klein, and Smith—but Red Willis wasn't letting anyone take a toehold at the plate. He dusted them back with just enough wildness to be effective. Once again it was one, two, three for the Bears.

Something happened to the Hedgetown fans then to transform each of them into a miniature Gabby Breen; at least Chip thought so. He'd never seen such a sight. Red Willis, bat trailing in the dust, stalked out to bat. Pandemonium broke loose. The Raptors' dugout erupted with yelling and whistling, while both Gabby Breen in the third-base coaching box, and the coach at first base seemed to go into hysterics. The fans got in on the noisy action, hurling remarks and clanging seats amongst their frenzied cheers. Chip held his hands over his ears and leaned forward to watch the effect upon Mills. He was glad *he* wasn't out there in the middle of all that confusion and bedlam.

Before the game, in the locker room, Kildane had sauntered over to Duer and told the manager he felt great and hoped he'd have the chance to put the Raptors where they belonged—below the Bears in the standings. But Duer had brushed him off, telling him that he was resting out the series.

"But I'm on, Eddie," Kildane had protested. "This is one of the big ones to win. Let me get it for you!"

Kildane talked in vain. Duer had made up his mind. "Not today, Scissors," he said kindly. "Maybe tomorrow." He then sent the tall pitcher out to the bullpen.

DUGOUT JINX

When the Bears took the field for the bottom of the second, the bullpen phone buzzed and Kildane dove for the receiver. "Here I go!" he quipped.

But Kildane was wrong. Duer wanted Burns to warm up. Dante Burns was a control pitcher, and Duer figured he might silence the Raptors' bats after Mills's wildness. But he was still hoping Mills might settle down.

"It's for you, Dante," Kildane said, turning to the husky hurler. "Eddie says you're next."

Kerrigan, the big pinch hitter who doubled as a relief catcher and outfielder, stood up and punched the catcher's glove. "Come on, Dante. Let's get those guys."

"Sure hope Windy settles down," Burns grunted. "These guys murder soft stuff in this park. Scissors is the only one we got who can handcuff 'em in this place."

"It's sure strange," Kerrigan said. "Windy's fastball usually works against them at home."

Unfortunately, Mills didn't settle down. Before Burns had tossed a dozen warm-up throws, Windy had passed Red Willis as well as the Raptors' leadoff hitter, Butch Bates. Duer called time, but he didn't take Mills out of the game. He sent the rangy pitcher out to left field and waved Bill Dawson out of the game. Dawson trotted back to the bullpen and sat down.

"Here we go," Dawson said fearfully. "Eddie's goin' to try Dante, and if he doesn't click, he'll use Windy again. Windy's through! He's used up for today. These Hedgetown fans are tough, and they've got the Raptors playin' for blood. This isn't baseball, it's murder! You see Willis throwin' those brushbacks?"

The first hitter Burns faced was Sandy Adams, a block of granite who played third base for the Raptors and hit second in the batting order. Burns kept them high, anticipating the bunt, but he had to bring it in when the count reached three and one. Adams pushed a perfect roller down the third-base line. Hale swooped in on the ball like a hawk, fielding it flawlessly, saw the runners were too far along for a successful force, and then threw Adams out by twenty feet. Still, Willis and Bates were in scoring position on third and second, and there was only one away.

Nick Marreno, the Raptors' first baseman, worked Burns to the three-and-one count and then blasted a hard-liner to the wall in right center. Willis and Bates scored as Ted Smith took the rebound from the wall. Marreno rounded second when the husky Bears right fielder set himself for the throw. The ball beat the Raptors' flying first baseman to third by fifteen feet.

Hale took the throw and poised behind the bag for the tag. Marreno came right on, making no attempt to slide. Instead, he charged head on into the little 150-pounder. Hale catapulted backward as though hit by a truck and landed on the back of his head. The ball flew up in the air, and Marreno cast a merciless laugh at Hale as he jogged home to score.

Eddie Duer reached home plate at the same time, tearing out of the dugout, dashing for Marreno just as he crossed the plate. Duer grasped the burly opponent and nearly jerked the giant's arm off as he spun him around.

In a second they were entwined while players from the field and the dugout joined in the melee. The umpires broke it up almost as soon as it started, but the heated argument that followed resulted in Eddie Duer's ejection from the game. Somehow Chip found himself right behind Duer and right in the center of things when the scuffle started, but he was never able to figure out how he got there.

DUGOUT JINX

Gabby Breen got a hero's ovation as he stomped back to the third-base coaching box, a broad grin of satisfaction on his face. Marreno's reception by the fans was less than enthusiastic. Even the Hedgetown fans found little excuse for his deliberate charge. Nevertheless, winning was still their main focus. Duer took his time about departing, and the crowd booed him every second he was in sight.

Bob Reiter took charge of the Bears and spent a long afternoon juggling pitchers, fielders, and hitters while trying vainly to stem the hitting assault by the Raptors.

At last the painful game was over for the Bears, and the Hedgetown fans howled enthusiastically for their "new team" and "fighting manager." They promised everybody, particularly the Bears players, they'd be back the next afternoon to see a repeat performance. They slowly left the scene of the massacre, howling and jeering the Bears as they pointed to the 16-3 score glowing on the scoreboard in center field.

The Raptors players continued their celebration in the locker room, cheering Red Willis and Nick Marreno. Breen was all over the place, patting the players on the back, playing up to them, and assuring them they'd give the Bears the same treatment the next afternoon.

"Just keep your eyes on me out in the third-base coaching box when you're up there. That's all you gotta do!"

The Raptors had responded to Breen. He wasn't the kind of man they might have chosen for a manager, but he'd brought them success today against their bitter rivals.

Actually, most of the Raptors players had been surprised at the choice of Breen. A few had been disappointed, but they all hoped the change might reverse the bad luck that had dogged them all year. Tonight, flush from the victory and the heartwarming support of the fans for the first time in weeks, they thought this game signaled the changing point, the hurdle that might mean the pennant.

Hunter Kearns was nearly as exuberant as his players. The near-record turnout and the play of the Raptors had lifted his spirits, and he dismissed some of his nagging worries about the new manager. That accounted for the big smile he flashed Breen in the office.

"Nice start, Gabby," Kearns said with approval.

"Thanks, boss. I told you we'd win, didn't I?"

"You sure did! By the way, Gabby, I thought Willis was throwing a little too close to the hitters, and I didn't like the melee Marreno stirred up when he charged into Hale."

"You're right on both counts, boss," Breen agreed. "I spoke to both of them about it."

"They're both a little hard to handle, especially Willis. Don't let them get out of hand."

"Don't worry, boss. I'll run the club."

"I hope so. You've made a good start. Keep it up!"

"Boss, you don't mind a little aggressiveness, do you? A winner's gotta be a fighter, you know."

"Well, the right sort of aggressiveness is all right, but I don't go for fighting. Let's win playing baseball and leave the fighting to the boxers. OK?"

Breen was smirking with satisfaction as he strutted to his car. He sure could pull the wool over Kearns's eyes. Of course you had to "yes" someone like Kearns, but that was easy enough. What a day! Everything had clicked. Now if he could only win tomorrow. Duer would probably start Kildane, and that big flagpole was tough. "The Squill treatment oughta take care of Kildane's fastball," he muttered happily. "Now, for a celebration dinner and then I'll wait for Corky."

The Bears were a sad, disgusted crew that night. The usual dining-room banter and laughter were absent. Chip felt as down as the rest. He hadn't liked the kind of baseball he'd seen today. All evening he tried to think of something else, but he couldn't get Corky Squill out of his mind. He kept going back to the same question that had disturbed him all afternoon: Why had Corky Squill suddenly changed from a sullen, morose loner to a peppy chatterbox?

At a nearby table, Dante Burns, Windy Mills, and Mickey Curry were talking, and without really intending to, Chip listened. Their words registered as clearly as the peal of a bell.

"They sure teed off on me!" Mills said worriedly. "Seemed to know every time I was gonna use my fastball. I don't get it! They never dug in on me before."

"I don't have much of a fastball," Burns admitted lamely, "but every time I threw one, they knocked the cover off it."

"We gotta take those guys tomorrow," Curry growled. "Some club! Manager heckling, pitcher beanballing, base runners playin' football. Hah! Marreno's going to run into something he won't like the next time he scores on me!"

Kildane swung around in his chair. "You can expect that kind of baseball from the Raptors from now on," he said bitterly. "The manager sets the pace, you know."

On the way out of the hotel dining room, Kildane stopped at Hale's table and placed his hands on the little third baseman's shoulders. "Feeling all right, Pauly?" he asked.

Hale nodded. "Neck's a little stiff, but otherwise I'm OK. Never figured he was going to charge me deliberately. I won't let it happen again!"

A MELEE AND A MASSACRE

"That's for sure," Kildane said grimly.

There was no movie for Chip and Kildane that night. They took their usual after-dinner walk and then headed back to the hotel.

"I want to get a good night's rest, Chip. See you in the morning. Night!"

Chip knew what his tall friend had in mind. Scissors was burning, and he was hoping Eddie Duer would let him work the next day's game. Chip hoped so, too, for several reasons. He'd studied Scissors Kildane's motions and pitches until he knew them by heart. Tomorrow's game would be a good time to verify something that had been running through his mind all evening. He decided to call his mom and the guys at the Sugar Bowl and then hit the sack too.

Most of the Bears players had gone to the movies, but a few lounged around the lobby reading and talking. The Bears played for keeps on and off the field. Eddie Duer was a gentle taskmaster, as long as his training and playing rules were observed. But woe to anyone who broke those rules! Duer was a tyrant where food and sleep were concerned. He believed a ballplayer was just as good as his food and rest. The Bears had the most liberal food allowance in the league, and his twelve-o'clock curfew was an absolute.

Corky Squill was missing from the lobby, but he would've been pleased by the conversation of the Bears players gathered there. In fact, Corky's play on the field that afternoon had been about the only Bears performance worth remembering.

"What's up with Corky?" someone asked.

"Got me," Damon Boyd said quizzically. "I've played next to him nearly two years now, and I've never heard him open his mouth before."

"He sure was a chatterbox this afternoon," Hale said, shaking his head. "You think Willis made him mad?"

"Could be," Stretch Johnson said thoughtfully.

"Corky would be the best second baseman in the league," Curry said appraisingly, "if he hustled every day like he did this afternoon. I never could figure out why he always clammed up when everyone else was pepping it up."

"Yeah, that's right," Boyd added. "I remember the time Eddie hauled him over the coals, tried to get him to do a little talking, and Corky just stood there as if he were mute, never said a word. Eddie finally got disgusted and left him alone."

"He's hard to crack," Johnson said wryly. "I guess I know Corky Squill better than anyone else on the club, but we're still strangers. I wish I could figure him out."

At that very moment Corky Squill was talking with Gabby Breen. Perhaps *listening* would be more accurate. Squill hardly had a chance to get in a word. Breen was wound up—excited, exuberant, and as usual, careless with the truth.

"Kearns was so happy he promised me a bonus. Imagine that! The first day! I told you he was that kind of a guy! Wait till you're on the payroll, you'll find out. What a start! And you know what? He told me right after the game that the Bears would be just an ordinary ball club without you and Mickey Curry. Of course, he also mentioned Kildane. So how's that?"

Squill nodded and started to speak, but the first word was barely formed on his tongue when Breen was off again.

"He's comin' around to our way of thinkin', Corky—fast! All you gotta do is keep up the good work. You looked great out there today. You can clinch him tomorrow. All he talked about besides the win was your playin'."

While Breen talked, he watched Squill closely. He had noticed the surly second baseman's coolness at the initial greeting and was utilizing all his persuasive talking powers to disarm Squill before giving him a chance to talk. Eventually, however, Breen talked himself into a spot, which gave Squill an opening.

"How did ya like Willis today?" Breen demanded proudly. "Had his stuff, didn't he?"

"Yeah, he had his stuff, all right," Squill retorted. "I shoulda parted his hair with a bat in the third when he threw his fastball at my head. Was that beanball stuff your idea or his?"

"Not mine, Corky," Breen quickly assured the irate player. "I don't go for that kind of pitchin' unless the hitters ask for it by crowdin' the plate. Eddie musta been boilin'!"

Squill nodded. "He sure was! In fact, the whole club's hot! I don't feel too good about you guys myself, and you might as well know it now as any other time. I'm not gonna take that beanball stuff from anyone, and that goes double for Willis."

Breen was thoroughly alarmed. He couldn't afford to have Corky get out of line now. So he turned on all his charm, paid for their meals, and went to work. When Squill left just in time to beat Eddie Duer's curfew, Breen and his former protégé were again on friendly terms.

CHAPTER 12

Dugout Jinx

CHIP HILTON was a completely normal teenager. He had ambitions beyond his college days, but along with those, he also wanted to excel as an athlete. Chip was smart enough to know that, other things being equal, the best competitor was the athlete who was well conditioned and able to give his best performance at critical times. That was why Chip was careful to eat sensibly and get plenty of rest.

Usually his day was so action packed that he had no trouble falling asleep as soon as his head hit the pillow. But that hadn't been the case during the past week. The travel, change of scenes, new faces, and excitement that accompany a team on the road had disrupted his normal way of life. Then there was Corky Squill. The Bears' pivot star's attitude toward him occupied Chip's thoughts every night, and tonight was no exception.

Chip tossed and turned, trying to figure out Squill's sudden change of attitude. Corky had been exceedingly friendly until the day of the race. Chip thought back, trying to understand why the mere loss of a race would cause such a change. It didn't make sense. Then he remembered that Squill's attitude had changed even before the race.

It had been obvious that something was wrong when Corky didn't answer when Chip spoke to him on the way to the outfield. Corky must have heard him; he wasn't more than ten feet away. Chip remembered saying, "Hi ya, Corky. I'm backing you up," and Squill had deliberately turned his back. So something must have happened even before that.

Chip's thoughts unaccountably shifted to Gabby Breen, and he began to wonder if Squill's animosity had anything to do with Breen's contract. That didn't make much sense either, except that the two men were friends. This thought started Chip off on another tangent, and it was hours before he finally dropped off to sleep.

Most of the Bears players slept late the day of a game and ate brunch before going out for hitting and fielding practice. Chip got up early, but he always waited for Kildane to come down to the lobby so he could eat with his friend. Today, he had time to read the story of the previous afternoon's game in the Sunday *Courier*. As he expected, the Raptors got a great write-up.

Raptors Maul Bears 16-3
Raptor Hitters Take Batting Practice
on Bears Pitching

Nick Marreno's grand slam homer and the near-perfect pitching of left-handed Red Willis were highlights of the Raptors' surprise mauling of the league-leading Bears yesterday afternoon. The victory was a nice welcome for the Raptors' new manager, Nelson

"Gabby" Breen, and provided local fans with new pennant hopes.

Willis was dazzling, limiting the visitors to four scattered hits while his teammates were amassing twenty-one safe bingles, nine for extra bases. Bears coach Eddie Duer, ejected in the bottom of the second, started Windy Mills, then shifted him to left field while Dante Burns gave it a try. Then Phil Akers lasted for two-thirds of an inning, while Troy Richards hung on for two. The Bears finally ended up back with their starting pitcher, Mills.

Marreno stepped to the plate with two aboard in the bottom of the second, and, on the three-and-one pitch, clobbered Dante Burns's pitch against the right center wall to score Willis and Butch Bates. Marreno scored on the play when Paul Hale dropped the ball in a collision at third.

Breen is expected to start Skids Baker this afternoon, but Eddie Duer was undecided early this morning about his choice. A win this afternoon might give the Raptors the momentum they need down the stretch. After today, the Raptors have ten more games to play, six against the Bears. It's conceivable the championship will be decided in the final home stand, a two-game series.

"Doesn't read too good, does it?"

Chip glanced up in surprise. He hadn't noticed Duer and Kildane, but when he saw who it was, he quickly jumped to his feet. "It sure doesn't," he said, smiling wryly.

"Throw that paper away and read tomorrow's story," Kildane said grimly.

Chip shot a questioning glance at the Bears manager. Duer nodded his head.

"Yep," he said lamely. "Scissors wouldn't let me come down for breakfast until I said he could pitch today. Come on. Let's get something to eat."

While they ate, Duer reviewed the Raptors' batting order for Kildane.

"You know Bates—bats right-handed, crowds the plate, waits 'em out, hits a fastball straight away. Doesn't like 'em around his wrists.

"Adams hits left, likes soft stuff, will pull everything except your screwball and an outside pitch.

"Marreno bats left, likes 'em around the letters, can't handle anything you throw around the knees.

"Castillo bats from the right side of the plate and takes a big cut. Mix 'em up, keep him off balance.

"Conover hits right, likes to dig in, takes a long stride. Can't handle the breaking balls.

"Roth bats right, pulls 'em, and is a sucker for the high inside pitch.

"Kinkaid is a cutie, crowds the right side of the plate, likes to wait 'em out. Can't hit the fastball.

"Berry will watch everything below his waist go by, especially fast stuff. He's a sucker for a sinker or anything resembling one.

"Baker couldn't hit a softball! Don't throw him a change-up.

"Well, that's it, Scissors. I guess you know 'em as well as I do. Wish you'd skip this game though. Take a rest. There's lots of time left, and we've got seven games with the Raptors."

Kildane would have none of that. Duer had said yes, and Scissors meant to hold the manager to his word.

On the way to the park in the bus, Kildane sat with Chip and again went through the Raptors' batting order. "Eddie always runs through the other club's batting order before a game," Kildane explained. "I guess you've heard him before. We do the same thing out in the bullpen while we're watching the game. That's usually Duster Reed's job. He's in charge of the bullpen, but he's in the hospital. Guess you didn't meet him. Might be back for the last game or so."

At the park, the Bears dressed quickly, anxious to get out on the field and get at the Raptors. Maybe it was this very eagerness that tightened them up, or maybe they tried too hard. At any rate, Squill, Boyd, and Dawson went down in order, just like the previous afternoon. When Scissors Kildane toed the rubber and faced the first Raptors hitter, Butch Bates, he got the same treatment the crowd had given Windy Mills. The crowd roar was one continuous jumble of sound.

"More batting practice!"

"Losers!"

"Boo, Bears!"

Before the game, Chip had watched the ball fly around the infield from Curry to Squill to Johnson to Hale to Boyd and back to Johnson, and he had felt a premonition, felt the strain the Bears had evidenced in the clubhouse. Nerves were stretched to the breaking point. It was obvious in the sharpness of their voices and the shortness of their tempers. It had struck Chip while he was dressing, and he'd tried to fade into the background, to keep quiet and remain as unobtrusive as possible.

No one had seemed to notice him except Corky Squill, who had waited until Duer left for the field to follow and hiss one word—"Jinx"—out of the side of his mouth as he passed.

Chip sat in the corner of the dugout now, watching Scissors go into his windup. The slender hurler had seemed right in his warm-up, firing the ball across the plate like a flash of light. As Chip turned his attention to the lead off hitter, Butch Bates, he saw Bates look at Gabby Breen in the third-base coaching box. Chip followed the glance and knew some sort of a sign had passed between them, but he hadn't been able to catch it. Before Chip could turn his head back to the plate, he heard the crack of the bat and saw the ball flying directly over second base. Bates had singled on the first pitch!

The Raptors fans were in a frenzy. They were already on their feet cheering Bates to the skies, while a crescendo of jabs flooded out toward Kildane.

The single hadn't upset Kildane. He stood just behind the mound, the resin bag in his fingers, looking down the alley at Mickey Curry. As he stepped to the rubber and took his stretch, Chip had again caught the left-handed hitter, Adams, watching Breen in the third-base coaching box. Chip figured the play was a sacrifice. So did Kildane. The ball came in fast and hard and across the shoulders on the outside for a called strike. Scissors wasted two and then evened the count with a curve that broke right across the middle. It was two and two.

Adams stepped out of the batter's box then and glanced down the third-base line at Breen. However Breen was looking out toward the outfield, and Adams reluctantly stepped back up to the plate.

Curry gave Kildane the sign, and Scissors toed the rubber. Chip was watching Adams like a hawk and caught the look he gave Breen, but Chip was too late to catch the sign, if there was a sign. He did see Adams step into the pitch, high outside, and send the ball bounding behind the runner between Squill and Johnson.

Stretch made a try but was a step too far away. Chip groaned, then leaped to his feet with a cry of excitement. Corky had darted far to his left, scooped up the ball with his glove, pivoted, and threw to Boyd scampering across the keystone bag to catch Bates by a step. Then Boyd made one of those impossible throws, clawing the air with his feet and throwing from his precarious position above the sliding Bates. The ball beat Adams by a whisper, and the umpire jerked his thumb over his shoulder. It was as nifty a double play as anyone would ever want to see. Even the Hedgetown fans responded with a scattering of applause.

Chip breathed easier. That was more like it! Still, he knew Bates and Adams had both hit the ball solidly, too solidly for comfort. Nick Marreno stalked up to the plate, scowling and thumping his bat on the ground. The crowd cheered, and Chip shot a quick glance at Kildane. He could tell by the expression on his friend's face that he was out to get the burly first baseman. Chip remembered Duer's warning: "Marreno likes 'em around the letters, can't handle anything you throw around the knees."

Marreno glanced at Breen in the coaching box and then stepped to the plate. Kildane whipped a fastball smack across the middle for strike one. The ball had been right at the knees. The next pitch was a curve that swooped across the inside corner for a called strike two.

"Atta boy, Scissors, strike him out! Can't hit 'em if he can't see them!" Squill's blast carried clear into the dugout, and Chip eyed the second baseman in astonishment. Corky was in front of second base waving his arms and jumping up and down as though he were crazy. He was still there when Kildane smoked his fast one low and outside for ball one.

"Right in there!" Squill boomed. "Put on your glasses, ump!"

The umpire's response was to call time and stalk out to the side of the plate and call Eddie Duer. Chip couldn't hear what was being said, but Duer went out behind the mound and talked to Squill. Corky waved a contemptuous hand at the umpire and moved back to his normal position.

"Claims Corky's obstructing the vision of the hitter," Duer said briefly, as he dropped down into the dugout.

"Move him out of there, Scissors," Squill yelled. "Give him a taste of his own medicine."

Marreno stepped out of the box and glared angrily at Squill. If he expected to squelch Corky with a look, however, he was disappointed. Squill placed the thumbs of his hand and his glove beside his ears and wiggled his fingers. The gesture infuriated Marreno, and Kildane's knee-high slider set the burly first baseman down on a called third strike.

Marreno whirled on the plate umpire's "s-t-e-e-r-i-k-e," and it seemed for a second as if he meant to attack the umpire. Shouting at the top of his voice, Marreno shook the bat menacingly at the impassive man in blue and protested the decision.

Corky came trotting in, again wiggling his fingers beside his ears, and Marreno nearly exploded. Squill simply kept going, laughing at the infuriated man, and the interruption served to distract Marreno's attention from the umpire. Relieved from the tension, the Bears came hustling into the dugout yelling and determined to "go get some runs!"

Skids Baker, a right-hander, was fast and equipped with a darting slider and a sharp curve. When he was right, he was tough—and he was right today. Squill topped one of the swooping curves, and it dribbled down the third-base line. Bates threw him out easily. Boyd struck out, and Dawson lifted a high fly to right field. It was three up and three down before Kildane hardly had time to snuggle into his jacket and mop his brow.

DUGOUT JINK

The Raptors continued their sharp hitting in the second, third, and fourth. Luckily, as in the opening frame, a Bears infielder or outfielder was in the right spot each time. Kildane said nothing, but Chip could tell he was worried by the consistent ring of the Raptors' bats.

Skids Baker, on the other hand, was having one of his big days. The husky hurler was fast and right, and the Bears' hitting had been limited to one safe bingle, a screaming liner in the fourth by Corky Squill, which was good for three bases. Unfortunately Squill had died there; his teammates hadn't gotten the ball out of the infield.

In the bottom of the fifth, Kildane's luck deserted him. Corey Berry, the Raptors receiver, led off with a sharp single, meeting one of Kildane's fastballs right on the nose. Chip caught the look of astonishment on Kildane's face and the warning glance Mickey Curry flashed toward Eddie Duer in the dugout. Then Skids Baker crossed up everyone in the park. Kildane played him for the advance, but the big pitcher met the high, fastball flush, pushing a looping liner to short right field.

Kildane really tried on Butch Bates, but the stocky shortstop, hitting from the first-base side of the plate, connected on a fastball, sending it inside the right-field foul line all the way to the fence. It was a perfectly placed hit—behind the runners on first and second—and good for a double, even though Ted Smith had played the pull-hitter correctly.

Berry and Bates scored, and the Hedgetown fans nearly tore down the stands. It didn't stop there. Sandy Adams walked, and Nick Marreno evened his score with Kildane by golfing one of Scissors's fastballs into right field for a clean single, scoring Bates and sending Adams to third. Jack Castillo followed and blasted a worm burner along the third-base line, which Hale miraculously knocked down. Adams started home but scurried back when Hale recovered the ball. So the bases were loaded with none away, and Duer called time and hurried out to the mound.

Chip could see Kildane shaking his head while Duer talked, and he knew his friend didn't want to be relieved. The Hedgetown fans added fuel to Kildane's fire of determination by booing and heckling. This was the first time in two years that the Raptors had been able to shake the confidence of the Bears' pitching star, and the crowd ate it up. They gave Eddie Duer a good going over, too, when he made his way back to the dugout. Bob Reiter cast an inquisitive glance at the worried manager.

"Says he's OK," Duer said briefly.

"What did Mickey say?"

"Same thing! Can't understand it! Says Scissors is workin' beautifully. Putting them right where they ought to go—unless the hitting data we have on these guys is all wrong."

Chip concentrated on the next hitter, Pete Conover. Duer had said the Raptors' right fielder was a power hitter, took a long stride, and couldn't hit a curve. Conover disproved that statement on the first pitch. Kildane came in with his darting curve that dipped toward the bottom of the strike zone. Perhaps it would be more accurate to say it started to dip, because Conover stepped into the curve, and his bat crushed the ball right on the nose. There was a tense second of stillness while every eye in the park followed the flight of the ball. Then a great roar burst over the field as the ball cleared the left-field fence and disappeared. It was a home run!

CHAPTER 13

Bad News Bears

SCISSORS KILDANE had been a pitching phenom ever since he joined the Bears. The lanky fireballer had known one success after another. True, he'd suffered a few defeats, but the battles had been close, anybody's game right up to the bottom of the ninth. But he'd never been humiliated, never experienced the bitter frustration a pitcher knows when he has all his stuff, has good control and feels right, but he still can't get his pitches past the hitters. Kildane experienced it this day.

Chip suffered along with Kildane through the rest of the disastrous game. He mentally threw every pitch, and he felt the same disheartening aches when the Raptors hitters teed off and drove in run after run. He was swinging with every Bears hitter as they tried desperately to get some runs, but it was no use.

Chip was as glad as the Bears to escape to the clubhouse after their last time at bat in the ninth. He shot a despairing glance at the scoreboard and noted the seventeen hits and fourteen runs in the Raptors' column. Chip didn't need to read the Bears' totals. He knew them by heart.

In the home team clubhouse, the Raptors were jubilantly talking, shouting, and laughing.

"We poured it on them," Breen proclaimed loudly, "but good!"

"Guess we showed Kildane how good he really is," someone shouted.

"It's about time," another added.

"We've got 'em now," Breen declared. "We'll stomp the Bears every time! Wait and see! Like I said, all you guys gotta do is watch me when you're up at that plate."

Tim Murphy, the Raptors' first base coach, shook his head with admiration.

"You sure called 'em today, Gabby!" he chuckled. "I don't know how, but you sure did it!"

"Leave that to me," Breen said, basking in Murphy's praise. Then he grew serious. "All right, now. No game tomorrow, so no curfew tonight. But everyone be here tomorrow at four o'clock for our first road trip as a winning team! Let's take two from the Leopards!"

The Bears dressed in silence, the heavy atmosphere reflecting their discouragement. Although nobody said anything, everyone in the locker room felt sorry for Scissors Kildane. Kildane had shown he could take it; he had kept bearing down all the way. He'd stuck it out in the face of the Hedgetown fans' ruthless razzing all afternoon and had asked Duer to let him finish the game. Kildane was no quitter, and he wasn't looking for sympathy.

Eddie Duer was last off the field. He came hustling into the room showing none of the tension of the four straight losses. He spoke in soft, even tones with reassurance and confidence.

"Don't worry about it! We lost it, but we'll get the next ones! We're out in front, and we're going to stay there! We're home for two in a row starting Tuesday, and by the way, we'll work out tomorrow at three o'clock. Let's hustle. We're outta here—the sooner the better!

On the return bus trip, Chip sat beside Kildane, and Eddie Duer and Mickey Curry sat on the opposite side of the aisle. Nothing much was said until they were well out of Raptors country. Then Curry abruptly voiced everyone's thoughts.

"Seemed ready for every pitch! Dug in for the fastballs, stepped into curves, and watched all the bad ones go by. I don't get it!"

"Just as if they knew what was coming," Kildane added.

"You could be right," Duer said thoughtfully. "It's been done before."

"You mean the signs?" Curry asked.

Duer nodded. "Yes and no! Could be Gabby is stealing the signs, or it could be he's stealing them from you."

"Me?" Curry demanded.

"Yes, you or Scissors. Could be you hold your glove in one position for fastballs and in another position for curves. Or it could be Scissors if he's using a different windup for different pitches."

"I've been careful about that ever since I've been with you, Eddie," Kildane said earnestly. "I think about that every time I throw. Chip and I were talking about it a couple of days ago."

"I know, Scissors," Duer said kindly. "Don't worry about it. I was just thinking out loud. Personally, I don't think Gabby Breen's that smart. Could have been just one of those days.

"Every team has those days once in a while, when it seems even the umpires can't get 'em out. We've had 'em, and there's no reason the Raptors can't have 'em! Anyway, it's water over the dam."

Chip was still staring out the window at ten o'clock when team frustration gave way to sporadic snores. Usually the sound of the big tires on the interstate and the gentle movements of the bus carried him into a quick slumber, but this time his thoughts wouldn't be stilled. He kept thinking about the Raptors and the defeats and, strangely enough, about Gabby Breen.

Kildane's words kept running through his mind. "You know, Chip, they seemed to be ready for anything I threw. I don't get it! They never got a toehold on me before, but today they planted themselves in the batter's box just as if they were getting the signs."

Just as if they were getting the signs! The phrase came back again and again until the repetitive monotony eventually lulled Chip into a troubled sleep.

Three o'clock the following afternoon Chip was chasing flies in Bears Stadium. Eddie Duer believed in practice, lots of practice. His players worked hard, putting out in practice just as they were required to put out in the games. These kids were hustlers. Eddie Duer needled them just a bit before hitting practice. Not too much, because the perceptive field boss realized the importance of easing up on a beaten team and pouring it on a cocky, winning team.

"Maybe we ought to sharpen up those batting eyes," he said dryly. "Chip, take the hill. We'll hit in our regular batting order for five or six rounds. Mickey, put on your gear. Everyone, hit three and lay one down. Show me some speed when you circle the bases. Let's go!"

Chip was already loose and needed only a few warm-up pitches before Corky Squill tapped the plate with his bat. Squill sneaked a cautious glance over his shoulder to make sure Eddie Duer was out of hearing range and then drawled insolently, "Throw me that jinx ball, Outsider. I wanna knock it down your throat!"

Chip's face flushed scarlet, but he said nothing. Instead, he turned and dusted his fingers with the resin bag while he regained control of his emotions.

"All right, Rabbit Ears," Squill muttered again, "throw me that nothin' ball of yours!"

Mickey Curry thumped his big fist into the catcher's glove. "Lay off, Corky," he growled good-naturedly. "Leave the kid alone!"

Squill whirled around, his eyes flashing as he glared at the big receiver. "You keep out of this," he snarled.

"Take it easy, Corky," Curry said quickly. "You'll make the kid mad, and he'll strike you out."

"*Him?* Strike *me* out?" Squill ridiculed. "That'll be the day!"

The fiery second baseman stepped out of the batter's box and then glanced toward the dugout where Eddie Duer was talking to Bob Reiter. Then he scowled angrily in Chip's direction. "Come on, Bad News," he growled. "Let's see you strike me out!"

Chip ignored him, and a straight hard one split the plate.

"Right in there, Corky," Curry said softly. "What's the matter? Too fast?"

"You mean that was a fastball?" Squill retorted, laughing harshly. "Maybe Bad News oughta move closer."

Curry grunted and carried the ball out to the mound. "Strike him out, Chip," he said earnestly. "Show the little troublemaker up!"

But Chip wasn't interested in striking out Corky Squill or anyone else right then. Eddie Duer wanted his players to get hitting practice, and he had told Chip to lay the ball across the plate.

Chip smiled and shook his head. "Guess I'd better just throw them over like Mr. Duer said, Mickey," he said.

"OK Chip," Curry said resignedly, "but it wouldn't make anyone mad. Corky's askin' for it, and he oughta get it."

Squill banged three hard line drives into left center and then dropped a nifty bunt down the first-base line. He sent the bat slithering along the ground nearly to the mound as he dug toward first, leaving no doubt he was out to get the young intern.

With the exception of Scissors Kildane and Mickey Curry, the Bears players weren't taking sides in the argument, but they glanced at one another with concern in their eyes. Next to Scissors, Corky was the most important player in their lineup, and a feud between their star pitcher and the spunky infielder could mean a lot of trouble in their drive for the pennant.

The rest of the afternoon was routine, but tension broke out again that night in the hotel lobby. This time it was an open break between Kildane and the morose infielder. Squill was bitterly complaining to Stretch Johnson when Scissors walked out of the elevator with Chip.

"Outsiders don't belong on the bench," Squill said pointedly, swinging around just in time to stare into Kildane's eyes.

"Are you talking to me?" Kildane asked coolly.

"No, I'm tellin' you," Squill snapped. "Outsiders don't belong in the dugout, even if they are the 'go-fer' for the big shot of the club."

"I don't know any gophers and I don't know any big shots, Corky," Kildane drawled, "but I do know you're acting like a spoiled brat."

Squill's face flushed darkly. "Maybe you'd like to try to do somethin' about that," he snarled.

"Maybe I would, and maybe I will," Kildane drawled.

"What's the matter with right now?" Squill challenged.

But he was talking to Kildane's back. Scissors had turned away and had headed toward the door where Chip was standing. Without a word, the two friends trudged down the street toward their favorite movie theater. Their silence was more expressive than words. Both were embarrassed, and conversation was difficult.

Chip didn't enjoy the movie that night. In fact, he couldn't have told anyone much about it because he was trying to figure out the reason for Corky's sudden animosity. He was still trying to figure it out the next afternoon while the Bears were trampling the Bluejays 13-2.

All through the game he watched Corky. As the stout second baseman chattered away, hopping around without a care in the world, Chip tried to piece together the puzzle. He knew something had happened to change both Corky's attitude toward him and his behavior on the field.

"Come on, Troy. We're behind you, kid. Atta boy!"

The victory over the Bluejays had been a *must* win. The Raptors had carved out a neat 6-1 score over the Leopards to keep pace in the stretch race and give Breen his third straight victory as the new Hedgetown manager.

Breen was on top of the world, and when the last Leopards batter fanned to end the game, Gabby rushed to the phone. He knew the Raptors' owner would be in his office listening to the game.

"Hello, Mr. Kearns—Gabby! . . . Yes, sir, we had 'em all the way. . . . We're sure gonna try! . . . I'm plannin' on Baker for tomorrow. . . . Turner will go against the Bears on Saturday. . . . We've gotta win that one!"

Breen's face wore a satisfied look when he hung up the phone. Everything was coming together. The Raptors were only two and a half games behind the league leaders now, and if they could hang on until Saturday, Lefty Turner might continue his mastery over the Bears with his wild southpaw curves and dusters.

But the wily manager's luck changed the very next day. The Leopards pounded Baker for fourteen hits and downed the Raptors 7-3.

For the Bears, Eddie Duer gambled on Phil Akers, who came through beautifully, shutting out the Bluejays while his teammates bunched their hits to score six runs. The Bears were four games up in the win column over the Raptors.

There's nothing like a win or two to cheer up a ballplayer. Team victories and raising batting averages erase everything. Scissors Kildane was such a loyal team player that he was almost his old self again too, although he still couldn't forget the hammering by the Raptors.

"I can't understand it," Kildane said grimly to Chip. "It's the first time the Raptors ever hit me consistently."

"You think Coach might be right about Gabby Breen getting the signs?"

Kildane shook his head decisively. "No, I don't. Curry's like a statue behind the plate. No, it's not Mickey, and I don't think it's me. I even practiced in front of a mirror for two years so I'd use the same motion for every pitch!"

Chip carried the problem to bed and into his dreams that night but couldn't find an answer. Every thread of a solution unraveled, and every time his thoughts came to a blind alley, Corky Squill appeared waving a gigantic bat and grinning diabolically as he challenged Chip, "Strike me out, Bad News!"

The Bears were idle the next two days, but Eddie Duer had them out at Bears Stadium each morning. Thursday passed without incident. Chip was careful to give Squill plenty of room, but the tension between Kildane and Squill came to a head during the Friday morning workout. Manager Eddie Duer was caught right in the middle of the trouble. Chip was throwing batting practice, and Squill was baiting him every time Duer was out of hearing. Mickey Curry and Scissors Kildane retaliated by needling the infielder whenever his turn came to bat.

"Can't hit his own weight, Chip," Curry chortled.

"Show him a fastball and watch him duck!" Kildane added.

"No swell-headed kid's gonna strike me out," Squill retorted. "Come on, Jinx, throw me one of your high school pitches!"

Although Eddie Duer seemed completely oblivious to the brewing feud between Squill and Kildane, he'd seen the trouble coming. Duer's success as a baseball coach wasn't solely due to his knowledge of the game. His leadership, personality, and extensive use of sports psychology were his chief strengths. Deciding to confront the problem, he maneuvered around the field until the stage was set and then appeared on the scene just in time to hear Squill's remark.

He was worried, but his attitude suggested he considered it nothing more than ballplayer horseplay. Still, he noticed the infielder's belligerence as he moved into action.

"Go ahead, Chip," he called, "go ahead. I'm neutral, so I'll call the balls and strikes."

Duer walked briskly out behind the mound and the ribbing ceased. Chip was nervous. He felt awkward, and his heart wasn't in the chore, but he made up his mind to do his best. Mickey Curry called Chip halfway in to the plate and gave him the signs.

"One finger for your fastball, Chip. Two for your curve, three for your change-up. What do you call it, a blooper?"

Chip toed the rubber and blazed his fastball low and inside for ball one. Then Mickey signaled for a curve that Squill watched swoop in and across to even the count. Chip came back with his fastball, which flashed like lightning across the letters. He was ahead, one and two.

Another curve swept in, and Squill caught a piece of it, fouling it back to the screen. Then Chip blazed in a sidearm fastball that just missed the plate. His next pitch sizzled in again, just missing the inside corner and driving Squill back from the plate to make it the full count.

Squill was pale with anger, but he didn't lose his head. He didn't let it get the best of him. Instead, he was deadly serious, concentrating intently on Chip and the last big throw. The players on the field were just as intent, as if this were the final pitch of a tight World Series championship game!

Chip shook Curry off until Mickey called for the change-up. He knew Squill was right for that kind of pitch after the fastball and the curve, and his windup was fast and complete. The ball looped high in the air, catching Squill off balance. Halfway through his swing, Squill checked the bat and tried to slow down to meet the high, looping pitch Chip called his blooper, but Squill had gone too far. He could only lunge at the lazy floater as it dropped past his bat and into Curry's big glove for strike three.

Scissors Kildane broke the silence. "Nice going, Chipper. What's the matter, Corky? I thought no high school pitcher could strike you out?"

Squill whirled around and glared at Kildane for a split second. Then he hurled his bat straight at the tall pitcher. Kildane leaped sideways and twisted away, but the spinning bat thudded into his left side. The blow nearly knocked Kildane down, but he kept to his feet, clutching his ribs and doubling over in pain. There was a shocked silence, broken by Duer's angry words before he joined the throng of players surrounding Kildane.

"What's the matter with you, Corky? You crazy?" Duer shouted. "Get into the clubhouse and out of that uniform. You're suspended as of now. And that little display of temper will cost you five hundred dollars! And I mean to make it stick!"

Eddie Duer figured five hundred dollars and suspension was a stiff penalty. What he didn't know then was that Scissors Kildane had suffered two cracked ribs and would be out of action for at least a week, maybe for the rest of the season. Bad news for the Bears!

CHAPTER 14

Troubleshooter behind the Plate

CORKY SQUILL, sitting outside William Malloy's private office, apprehensive beads of perspiration dotting his forehead, could hear the mumble of voices and knew his baseball future was hanging by a thin thread. The news of Scissors Kildane's cracked ribs had spread through pennant-mad Parkville like wildfire. The rumors had spread, too, but the real story was the property of the Bears players, the coaching staff, and Chip Hilton. Eddie Duer had explicitly instructed that only the club's publicity staff would release any details.

Yes, Corky was perspiring and fretting, trying to build up a case against Scissors Kildane. But he was finding it difficult to justify his actions and shift the blame to the popular pitcher. If he could have heard Kildane right then, Corky would have been extremely confused. At that very moment, Scissors Kildane was pleading with Eddie Duer and the club owner, William Malloy, to forgive Corky Squill.

"Look, Mr. Malloy," Kildane said earnestly, "it wasn't Corky's fault. We'd been razzing him, and I guess I heaped it on heavier than I should have. Anyway, the way the Raptors are going, we're going to need every man, every game."

Eddie Duer's set jaw and the determined light in his eyes revealed he didn't go along with Scissors's plea. "I don't agree, Scissors," he said firmly. "Corky's been looking for trouble for the past two weeks—" Kildane started to interrupt, but Duer waved him into silence as he continued.

"I know exactly how you feel, and I appreciate your team spirit, but this is a disciplinary matter. Corky's got to grow up."

Kildane nodded. "You're right, Eddie, but I'm speaking for the team, and I know how they feel. We had a meeting and they appointed me spokesman. The whole crew wants to forget it."

Bill Malloy smiled. "I think I understand, Scissors," he said gently. "Suppose you leave it to Eddie and me to work out. OK?"

William Malloy knew exactly what had happened at the team meeting. So did Eddie Duer. They both knew Kildane had called the meeting, had taken responsibility for the trouble, and had convinced his teammates to let him defend Corky. For several minutes after Scissors left, the two men sat quietly. Field boss Eddie Duer broke the silence.

"What do you think, Mr. Malloy?"

What Bill Malloy thought took a long time to express. Two hours later Corky Squill knew the five-hundred-dollar fine would stick, and he knew he'd been reinstated only because Scissors Kildane had gone to bat for him.

Unfortunately, Corky Squill didn't have enough faith in his teammate to understand why. He just figured

Scissors Kildane was a wimp or was trying to protect the bonus he probably had at stake in the championship race. When Corky clambered aboard the team bus at five o'clock that afternoon, the only part of the incident that worried him was the loss of his five hundred dollars.

That night after the Bears checked into their hotel in Hedgetown, Squill hurried to the nearest phone to call Gabby Breen.

Breen greeted Squill's call gleefully. "Boy, are we lookin' good," he snickered. "Kearns is walkin' on air! . . . What d'ya mean lucky? . . . Say, what's the real story on Kildane? Rumors say he was hurt in battin' practice. You sound like there's more to it. By the way, Kearns thinks you're great. Give him a good show tomorrow, kid! . . . We're in! You looked great here last week. Kearns says you're a real chatterbox! . . . Sure it's what I want! Now, look! Call me next Tuesday. Be sure to put on a good show tomorrow."

Squill was feeling great when he slid out of the phone booth. This time next year he'd be with Breen, and the Bears, Eddie Duer, Scissors Kildane, and Chip Hilton would be nothing but a memory. If Hunter Kearns liked hustling, talk-em-up guys—wait until tomorrow afternoon!

The Hedgetown fans were running a pennant fever. Everybody in town knew the league-leading Bears were just three and a half games ahead of the hard-charging Raptors. All that could change. Fans jammed the gates two hours before game time so they could watch warm-ups and harangue the Bears players. And did they ever! They were a nuisance to everyone, particularly Scissors Kildane.

"Hey! Kildane! What happened? Forget to duck?"

DUGOUT JINX

"Real convenient, Scissors! Saves you from another loss!"

"You're all used up anyway, Kildane! The Raptors own you now!"

"Bye-bye, Teddy Bears! We're chasin' you right out of the race!"

The Raptors had pennant fever too! They trampled all over the Bears. In the top half of the fourth, with the Raptors leading 7-2, Corky Squill started to stomp back and forth in the dugout, griping about the jinx. Then he mixed up the bats, poured water on the handles, and generally put on a show.

Chip knew the display was chiefly targeted at him. He sat there, taking it all, quietly turning the other cheek, not saying or doing a thing. But he could and did watch Squill's antics on the field.

"Maybe he does this when he's mad, or nervous, or showing off," Chip murmured to himself. But Chip's better judgment told him that wasn't the answer. Squill was confident and skillful. He wasn't the kind to freeze up, to choke. As far as Chip could tell, Corky was at his best when the going got tough.

Kildane was out in the bullpen, his ribs bandaged, but he was in uniform and tossing the ball, grimacing each time. He remained there while his pitching mates tried in vain to dam the flood of Raptor hits. When the last Bears hitter struck out in the top of the ninth, Kildane walked slowly to the dugout and joined Chip.

"Don't understand it, Chip," Kildane said wearily. "We used to own these guys. I just can't figure it out!"

Chip wasn't trying to figure out the Raptors' sudden mastery of Bears pitching; he was trying to figure out Corky Squill. Against the Bluejays, the stocky infielder had gone back into his shell, played silently and without wasted motion. Today, he was like the Energizer Bunny—going, going, and going! He brandished his arms, kicked dirt with his spikes, charged in to the edge of the infield grass, shifted from side to side, and generally behaved like a whirling dervish.

Squill had been solid! In fact, he'd been the Bears' shining light, going three for four at bat and fielding his position flawlessly. It didn't matter much in the score however. The Raptors easily won the battle, overpowering the Bears with a 14-4 victory.

The Hedgetown fans were thrilled! They savored each victory, as did the players. Inside the clubhouse, the Raptors players roughhoused and yelled friendly insults at one another while Hunter Kearns and Gabby Breen sat in the manager's room, celebrating the victory.

"Nice win, Gabby," Kearns said happily.

"I told you we'd do it!" Breen boasted. "They're ours! With or without Scissors Kildane!"

Kearns didn't have a chance to talk much after that. Breen was bubbling over with joy and spewing like a volcano. "Five more games with those guys, three at Parkville and two here. Oh, man! The way we're goin' and with Kildane out, we might take it. If we can knock off two of the three in Parkville, we'll clinch the pennant.

"But how'd you like that Squill? What a second baseman! He would give us the best infield in the minors!"

Kearns nodded his head. "He's good! Got more hustle than anybody I ever saw."

"You shoulda seen him when I had him. Duer don't know how to handle him, and wants to get rid of him. I heard some of the Parkville fans talkin' about the trouble between him and Duer. That means we could get him cheap."

"Could be," Kearns murmured dryly, "but you can be sure Eddie Duer won't break up his infield until the season is over. Let's forget trades and players and everything for now except the pennant. I'm sure glad, as it turned out, that we were rained out of those early games with the Bears."

"Me too!" Breen agreed. "Those rain outs are gonna mean the pennant for us!"

Eddie Duer had no idea what Kearns and Breen were talking about, but he was thinking the same thing. Except for the early season rain, these last three defeats by the Raptors wouldn't have been possible. Dressing slowly, he was thinking back through the season when his young team had been tearing up the league. Now he was worried.

The Raptors' sudden surge and their surprising domination of his team puzzled him. He knew a change of managers often resulted in a sudden lift in the spirit and play of a club, but he couldn't understand why it should affect another club's play. Especially his! But it had. There was no getting around it. The Bears had lost their confidence against the Raptors.

Chip sensed that too. The Bears were a defeated club in spirit and in the win-loss column. He glanced cautiously around the room. Subdued voices replaced the usual banter and boisterous needling, and on the bus that night, talk centered around one subject—the Raptors.

"Just don't get it! Some of those guys can't hit their weight, but they knock us out of the park."

"They've been teeing off the last three games!"

"Something's wrong!"

"Well, we won't get anywhere looking over our shoulders," Eddie Duer remarked pointedly. "What's done is done. Let's take the Hornets tomorrow and then think about the Raptors."

The Bears took the Hornets, all right, sending three pitchers to the showers and pounding out a confidence-building 11-3 win. Their spirits rose sharply, too, when the lowly Comets took the overconfident Raptors 2-1. That restored the Bears' lead to three and a half games and put all the burden of winning the pennant on the Raptors.

Chip had concentrated on Corky Squill during the game and was more puzzled than ever. Against the Hornets, Squill had again made a complete reversal; he had retreated once more into his shell. He remained in his shell during the Monday practice, sphinxlike in his play and in his behavior toward his teammates.

The Parkville fans were faithful and out in force to help their beloved Bears meet the Raptors' pennant threat Tuesday afternoon. This three-game series in the hometown park was the crucial series. The Bears had five more games to play, all with the Raptors. The Raptors had six games to play. The pennant could be won in the next two days!

Chip slipped away when Kildane was surrounded by a group of young fans wanting autographs outside the ballpark and hurried to a ticket window. He bought a ticket for a seat right behind the plate. Just before game time, he moved unobtrusively out of the dugout and through the gate leading to the stands. Most of the fans knew him and several spoke to him. Chip felt out of place in the stands wearing a uniform, and almost turned back. But he was determined to check out something once and for all, and the seat behind the plate was important.

DUGOUT JINX

Eddie Duer started Windy Mills, and the Raptors started swinging from their heels with the first pitch. The Bears didn't get them out until four runs had scored and a dejected Mills was under the shower. Akers relieved Mills with two down and the bases loaded, but only a storybook up-against-the-fence catch by Ted Smith in right field saved the day.

Chip was concentrating on Corky Squill every second the Bears were in the field. It required concentration because Corky was again a human dynamo, pepping it up and hustling, moving back and forth continuously.

Innings later, in the confusion of the home team stretch and with the Raptors leading 8-0, Chip made his way through the standing fans and back into the dugout. He hadn't even been missed. Chip was glad for that. At last he thought he knew why the Parkville hurlers couldn't get the visitors out. He'd know for sure tomorrow!

The Parkville fans weren't worried, but their pride was hurt by the ease with which the Raptors were handling their heroes. The Raptors had now won four in a row from the Bears. It just didn't figure.

"We'll take 'em tomorrow, all right!"

"We'd have the pennant won if Kildane hadn't been hurt!"

"Something funny about that. Never did hear the real story about how he got hurt!"

"No one else has either," someone observed. "I think Eddie Duer ruined his arm—used him too much and is covering up for it."

The Bears players began to show the effects of the strain too. The 8-0 lacing that afternoon had added to the building tension. Like the fans, they began to think the pennant might have been all wrapped up if Scissors

Kildane had been available. Not that they doubted their ability to take the series and with it the pennant, but the Raptors seemed to be getting all the breaks.

Wednesday afternoon brought disaster. The Raptors did it again! The pennant-hungry predators unleashed a savage hitting attack. They scored an easy nine runs, driving every available Bears pitcher to the showers. The hometown forces could muster only three scattered tallies. The Parkville lead had been cut a full game, and for the first time, the confidence of the Bears fans, the players, and Eddie Duer was shaken.

Chip Hilton's confidence was shaken too. Once again he had slipped out of the dugout to watch the game from behind the plate. What he saw convinced him he held the key to the Raptors' domination of the Bears' pitching.

Scissors Kildane wasn't very talkative that night at dinner and stirred his ice cream until it melted. Finally, only he and Chip remained in the room. It was just as well because Chip was deeply involved in his problem. No matter how he tried, he always came back to Kildane. He decided to get it off his chest.

"Scissors," he began slowly, "could we sit behind the plate tomorrow during the game?"

Kildane looked at him in surprise. "In the stands?" he repeated. "No way, Chip. I've got to stay with the team. This is the stretch, and I belong in the bullpen."

"You can do more in the stands, Scissors. Look, I've got two tickets right behind the plate. You sit with me for two or three innings, and you'll learn something important."

"Like what?"

"Like why the Raptors hit so well against us."

Kildane stared at Chip in surprise. "What's sitting in the stands got to do with it?"

"Well, for one thing you can tell whether or not I'm right when I call the pitches."

"Call the pitches?" Kildane echoed. "You mean you can call the pitch before Akers and Mills and Richards and the rest of us throw?"

"I think I can. I called them yesterday and today."

Kildane's eyes widened in astonishment! Behind the shock of surprise, his mind was working with lightning speed. Disbelief had been his first reaction, but he'd come to know Chip Hilton. He knew his young friend was sensible and sound, unlikely to make this kind of statement unless he was sure of his ground.

"How? How can you tell?"

"I'd rather not say, Scissors."

"But if you can call the pitch, Chip, maybe someone else can too. Maybe the Raptors can tell! They sure act as though they know what we're going to throw. Come on! We gotta see Eddie!"

Chip shook his head vigorously. "I won't tell Mr. Duer anything, Scissors. I'd tell you first, if I was going to tell anyone. I can prove it's possible, but you'll have to figure the rest out yourself."

"But why, Chip? Suppose the Raptors know! They'll win every game!"

Chip was adamant. He wasn't going to tell anyone what he suspected. Even if he knew for a certainty he was right, he wouldn't tell.

CHAPTER 15

Double-Cross Signs

SCISSORS KILDANE in the stands? That was something! The fans sitting around the popular pitcher recognized him immediately, greeting him with affection and enthusiasm.

"Hey, Scissors! Won't they let you in the dugout?"

"How you feel? We gonna take 'em today?"

"Who's working? How's the ribs?"

"Hey, Hilton. How ya doin'?"

Kildane was everybody's friend, and he answered every question, but he didn't neglect the task at hand. His midnight talk with Eddie Duer had been lengthy and thorough. The worried manager had been doubtful, but he wasn't overlooking the possibility that Chip had uncovered something worth considering.

"Chip's pretty observant and knows baseball, Scissors. He may have caught something we've overlooked. You know, there's something not quite right about the way the Raptors have been teeing off on us."

"You're telling me!" Kildane said wryly.

"Anyway," Duer continued, "there's nothing to lose, and if Chip's been clever enough to figure it out, let's check it out."

Scissors Kildane was all for it. Appearing carefree, he responded with enthusiasm to the fans but concentrated on Chip Hilton.

Troy Richards was clever. His delivery was as tricky as his stock in trade, and his all-time record against the Raptors stood at nine wins against two defeats. But today something was wrong. When he threw a curveball, the hitter stepped into it, met the ball before the break. When he fired a fastball, the batter leveled off and swung with power and confidence. Troy couldn't understand it. Neither could the fans.

Eddie Duer knew the Raptors hitters almost as well as his own. He knew the pitches they liked and those they didn't. Mickey Curry knew the Raptors just as well and worked Richards perfectly. But it was no use. His frustrated glances to Duer each time he hustled into the dugout expressed his feelings far better than any words.

Behind the plate, in the stands, a shocked and incredulous Scissors Kildane heard Chip call every pitch as accurately as if he could read Mickey Curry's mind. Curry would squat, flash the signs to Richards, and right then, almost as quickly, Chip would whisper "fastball" or "curve" or "change-up."

Kildane checked each pitch and then tried to figure it out. He knew it was a waste of time, but he checked Curry anyway. The veteran receiver never varied his actions, giving the signs with the fingers of his hand pressed closely against the inside of his right leg in the squat. Still, by the time he fixed his big glove as a target, Chip had already called the next pitch.

"Nope," Kildane muttered, "it isn't Mickey. It's gotta be Richards!"

But it wasn't Richards, at least Kildane couldn't see any hint in Troy's delivery. In desperation, he checked beyond the center-field fence, half expecting to see, even at that distance, someone with a pair of binoculars and a mirror flashing the signs. The idea was extreme, but he was determined to check every possibility. It was no use. Kildane finally admitted he was completely baffled!

"I don't get it, Chip. Look, you've just gotta tell me. This is serious."

"I'm sorry, Scissors. I can't tell you—I just can't!"

"But this is important, Chip. If you can get the signs, they can too—unless you're a mind reader."

"I'm no mind reader, and there's nothing particularly mysterious about it, Scissors. You can figure it out."

"How about Breen, Chip? He's in the coaching box. He got anything to do with it? You can tell me that much."

Chip deliberated briefly, then nodded. "Yes, he has, Scissors," he said firmly. "A lot to do with it. But that's all I'm going to say."

Kildane studied Chip with a long, penetrating glance. Then he nodded his head understandingly. "I get it, Chip," he said softly. "You're right! You're absolutely right. I won't bother you anymore about it. I think I know now why you can't tell me. Why don't you stay here. I've got to talk to Eddie. See ya after the game."

Kildane didn't pause to talk to the fans. He hurried down the steps and through the gate next to the dugout. A despairing glance at the scoreboard told him it was too late to do much about this game. It was the bottom of the eighth, and the Raptors were out in front, 11-2. But he could at least tell Duer that Breen was getting the signs somehow, someway, somewhere.

Eddie Duer hadn't given up. The fighting manager of the Bears was driving his players by word and example. He talked confidently to his faltering young players.

"Come on. Let's get on this guy! Where's the life in this dugout? What's a few runs! Come on, Damon, start it off!"

But the Bears couldn't get started; they couldn't even reach first. It didn't really matter that the Raptors got two more runs in the top of the ninth. The Bears were blanked again in their last time at bat. So the Raptors swept the series and cut the Bears' lead to half a game. That left the Raptors with three games to play, one with the Comets and the two final games of the season with the Bears at Hedgetown.

It had been a tragic series for the Bears and the Parkville fans. The three-and-a-half-game lead had looked big three days ago. Now it had practically vanished, and anything could happen, especially in the final two-game series at Hedgetown.

Scissors Kildane excitedly whispered the details of his enlightening experience in the stands to Eddie Duer, while the Bears were in the field in the top of the ninth.

"Can't be," Duer said doubtfully. "Chip knows our signs. So what?"

"Sure, we all know them, Eddie, but you can't see 'em up in the stands!"

"You're right! How in the world does he do it?"

"The only way I can explain it is that Chip knows by the motions," Kildane said ruefully. "Mine too, I guess."

Duer nodded thoughtfully. "Could be, but you know what that means? If Chip can figure our pitches, so can Gabby Breen and everyone else in the league. Particularly Breen!"

"Chip called every pitch, Eddie. I know it sounds weird, but it's true. He named them before the windup, and if he said 'fastball,' it was. And when he said 'curve,' it was! I checked every pitch, not just a few."

"And he wouldn't tell you how he knew the pitches?"

"Nope. Nothing, except Breen was mixed up in it."

"Did you watch Breen?"

"Sure, but he wasn't doing anything unusual that I could see. He was giving signals to their hitters and runners just like we do."

"You think he could see Mickey's signs?"

"No! Positively not! He didn't even seem to be looking at the plate when Mickey was giving his signs."

Duer shook his head worriedly. "Well, we're sure gonna do something about it as soon as this debacle is over. Nothing like this ever happened to me in all the years I've been in baseball."

Right after the game, Duer headed for Bill Malloy's stadium office, asking Bob Reiter to bring Mickey Curry and Scissors Kildane upstairs as soon as possible.

Bill Malloy was shocked by Eddie Duer's disclosure. Malloy had been in baseball a long time, never as a player but as an enthusiastic baseball fan and owner. When the first shock wore off, he began a clear analysis of the situation.

"It makes sense, Eddie!" Malloy declared. "The Raptors have taken us six in a row, and whether it's a coincidence or not, every one of those defeats occurred since Gabby Breen took over."

Duer echoed sourly. "We haven't given them a close game in a month."

"Of course," Malloy deliberated, "Chip could know Kildane and Richards and Mills and the rest of them so well that he might be able to figure out the pitch, especially if he knew the play situation and the hitters' weaknesses."

"But he said Breen was involved."

"That could be his own imagination. Breen undoubt-
edly flashes hit-and-take signs to each batter, and Hilton
may have picked those up."

"Could be," Duer agreed doubtfully, "but Scissors
said he called every pitch, never missed a single one."

"Doesn't seem possible. Why don't we bring Chip up
here?"

"Scissors said Chip wouldn't say how he could call
the pitches or anything else, except that Breen was the
key. He'd confide in Scissors before anyone else. The two
kids are firm friends, and you can bet he'd tell Scissors
if he was going to tell anyone. Hilton's a sensitive kid,
and we've got to remember his position. He's more or
less an outsider; we can't expect him to solve our grief."

"I guess you're right. Anyway, he's given us plenty to
work on. We can carry the ball from here. Let's leave his
name out of our discussion with Reiter and Curry. You
think Scissors told them anything?"

Duer shook his head. "No, I told Scissors not to
breathe a word to anyone."

"Good! We can keep Scissors out of it too. He'll understand."

"You can be sure of that. Another thing, if we keep
the two of them out of it, maybe Hilton will open up. He's
supposed to go home Saturday night for a few days
before heading off to college."

Malloy nodded. "We've got a job cut out for us. If the
Raptors win tomorrow, and there's no reason to think
they won't, we'll be all tied up."

"Well," Eddie affirmed, "we've got to figure out how
they're getting the signs, and we'll sure have to change
them."

Their conversation was interrupted by the arrival of
Bob Reiter with Scissors Kildane and Mickey Curry. The

three men entered the office uncertainly, but Bill Malloy immediately put them at ease, smiling warmly as he shook their hands.

"Sit down, men. Sorry to hold you up, but we're in the middle of something important. Eddie will bring you up to speed."

Eddie Duer's words flattened Bob Reiter and Mickey Curry like a twister. Scissors Kildane knew what was coming.

"Men," Duer said grimly, "the Raptors have been getting our signs!"

Varied emotions registered on the faces of Duer's listeners. Bill Malloy's eyes ranged from one face to another as he noted their reactions. Bob Reiter shook his head in astonishment. Mickey Curry's eyes blinked furiously and little knots of muscles gathered around his tightly clamped jaws. Then he nodded his head vigorously.

"I knew it!" he said through tightly pressed lips. "They had to! Their hitters were set for every pitch!"

Bob Reiter's speech came back in a rush of words. "No wonder we couldn't get 'em out! It didn't figure. Guys like Conover, Roth, and Kinkaid aren't known for cracking the ball every time they come up."

"And Berry and Baker," Curry added.

"Well, even I could hit if I knew every pitch that was coming," Duer said ruefully.

"How are they getting the signs?" Curry asked. "I know they aren't getting them from me! I've even been wearing an inner shirt with long sleeves so the muscles on my forearm wouldn't show when I gave the signs."

"That's nonsense!" Reiter exploded. "I never did believe a coach could steal signs by watching the muscles in a catcher's arm."

"It's not nonsense!" Duer said sharply. "We can't overlook a single possibility. The Raptors are getting the signs, and it means the pennant unless we can stop it."

"But how?" Curry insisted. "How are they getting them? How do we even know they're getting them?"

"We don't know how they're getting them, Mickey," Duer explained, "but you can take my word that they're getting every sign we throw. And if we don't solve it, we can kiss the pennant good-bye."

"Well, what's our next move?" Reiter asked.

"Change the signs for one thing," Curry said quickly.

"Maybe that won't be enough," Duer said ominously, wishing he didn't have to say the words.

A long silence followed. Each person in the room reluctantly explored the possibilities the statement implied.

Bill Malloy brought them relief from that repugnant thought. The owner of the Bears wasn't ready to accept that implication. "Changing the signs will be enough, Eddie," he said confidently. "You'd better work up two sets and check every possible leak. You can do a lot between now and Saturday."

"I'll have to!" Duer said shortly.

"You using me Saturday, Eddie?" Kildane asked quietly. "That's the big one, and Doc said I was ready to go."

"You're right, Scissors," Duer said grimly. "It's the big one—and you're pitching!"

CHAPTER 16

Playing for Second Place!

EDDIE DUER got busy that night working out a new set of signs. Nine o'clock found Reiter, Curry, and Kildane in Duer's room.

"We'll start practice tomorrow morning in the clubhouse at ten o'clock, going over the new signs, Bob," Duer said briskly. "And in the afternoon we'll work behind closed gates." Mickey nodded in approval.

Mickey Curry was an ideal leader. He was an experienced catcher, a fighter, and a team player. As the person chiefly responsible for the signs, it was only natural for him to take the lead in making suggestions. He leaned forward, now, speaking earnestly in his soft voice.

"We've been using two sets, Eddie. Maybe we ought to try an addition series and start our signs at six. That way, six would be a fastball, seven a curve, eight the change-up, and nine a pitchout."

"Might be OK," Duer agreed. "That means you can call for a fastball several ways. You can flash three fingers twice or two fingers three times, right?"

"Too complicated," Reiter laughed, shaking his head. "We don't have Al Einstein or Stephen Hawking playing for us."

"It's got to be complicated," Curry interrupted. "I've been working behind the plate for twelve years, and this is the first time I've ever had trouble with the signs. If they're getting the signs in spite of the way I've been protecting them—well, the more complicated the better."

Duer settled the issue. "We'll use Mickey's addition series," he said flatly. "Mickey, you work with the pitchers. Bob, you take Corky and Damon.

"One more thing, Bob. I want you to check on the way Corky and Damon flash the signs to the outfield. Check the outfielders too. Maybe Dawson, Klein, or Smith are shifting in some way on the relay or making some kind of movement.

"I know all this seems extreme, but with the pennant at stake, and with what we know, we can't afford to overlook a single possibility. Have we overlooked anything? Mickey, I want you and Scissors to stay here a little while longer. The rest of you can go."

Duer sat quietly after the others had left, looking from Scissors to Curry. Then he got up, locked the door, and sat down on the bed. He spoke in a near whisper.

"I hope what I'm about to say will never be repeated and never have to be used. But, as I said before, no possibility can be overlooked, and it may be necessary for us to disregard *all* team signs."

Curry was bewildered. "You mean you think some-one—"

"I mean that there's too much at stake to overlook *any* possibilities," Duer said firmly. "I want you two to have a special set of signs of your own."

"That means two sets at one time then," Curry said doubtfully. "One for the team and another for me and Scissors."

"Any other ideas?" Duer asked.

"Why can't I flash the signs for the hitter and have Mickey give the team signs?" Kildane queried.

"That would be better," Curry agreed. "Scissors flashed 'em to me in several games last year, and I relayed them to the guys. It'll work better if we have to use two sets."

"Maybe," Duer said thoughtfully. "But what about the others? They'll be playing for one pitch, and Scissors will be throwing another. Maybe it would be better if you didn't give any signs at all, Mickey. Yes, I think that's better. If things get that far, we'll cut out all team signs and let Scissors flash his signs just to you. Well, thanks. That's all. Get a good night's sleep."

Chip was lonely. Tonight was the first time he'd been entirely on his own since he'd taken the internship with the Bears. He finally ended up in a movie he wasn't enjoying. His mind was too filled with the pennant race, the signs, and home. This time next Saturday night he'd be on his way back to Valley Falls. Then, after a week at home, he'd be off to college—off to State and football.

Kildane was in bed when Chip got back to the hotel, but he wasn't asleep. The lanky pitcher was thinking about the big game on Saturday and the signs, and he wanted to talk.

"Chip, hit the lights. I'm not asleep. Where'd you go tonight? Movie? Man, this has been a long day. You know,

I still can't figure out how you can call the signs. Sure wish you'd tell me."

Chip shook his head. He hadn't and wasn't going to change his mind. Kildane sighed and changed the subject.

"Are you sure you have to leave Saturday night? Can't you wait until Sunday?"

"I can't stay, Scissors. I shouldn't have hung around this long. I'll listen to the game on the radio though."

Chip wished he was listening on the radio the next morning. He wished he was far away from Eddie Duer and the Bears players gathered in the clubhouse. They were thunderstruck by the manager's revelation about the signs.

"Men, the Raptors are getting our signs. That's why they've been able to hit us so freely the last couple of weeks. And one thing is for sure—they're stealing the signs or someone's tipping them off."

There was a deep silence as the impact of the ugly thought struck home. After a moment, Duer continued. "I'll rule the second part out right now. I know every player on this club, and I'd trust each of you with my life. But they're getting the signs, so that means they're stealing them.

"The only thing we can do is use two or three sets of signs. Starting tomorrow, we'll use different signs all through the game, maybe change every inning."

That afternoon, for the first time, the Bears workout was private, held behind locked gates. Two or three hundred fans had shown up and were keenly disappointed when they were turned away by the sudden change of policy.

By that evening, however, it seemed the whole town knew the Raptors had whitewashed the Comets 6-0 at

PLAYING FOR SECOND PLACE!

Alton. The race was all tied up with two games to go! A huge crowd stood outside Parkville's Bears Stadium to cheer the Bears as they boarded the team bus for the final two games of the season. The majority of the Parkville fans caught only a glimpse of their team favorites waving from the windows as the bus pulled away.

The next afternoon when Scissors Kildane toed the rubber and faced the first Raptor hitter in the bottom half of the initial inning, the owner of the Bears was seated beside Chip directly behind the plate.

"Chip, you don't have to tell me a thing," Malloy assured. "I just want to hear you call the pitches. I just can't believe it."

Chip could and did call the pitches. He called them correctly every time. Malloy was flabbergasted. Down on the field, Mickey Curry and Scissors Kildane were just as confused. Hits were ringing off the Raptors' bats as though it were batting practice. The first three Raptors hitters had singled, and the bases were loaded.

Chip had never been in the middle of a crowd like this one. Everyone was on his feet, and the crowd roared like the thunder of a hundred Niagara Falls.

Eddie Duer had called time and was talking to Kildane and Curry in front of the mound.

"You all right, Scissors? You sure you're all right?"

"I'm right, Eddie! I never felt better in my life!"

Curry agreed. "He's OK, Skipper, but it looks like they're still at it. They're set for everything he throws."

Duer shook his head grimly. "Well, change the signs again. That's all I know to do."

The plate umpire touched Duer with the mask he held in his hand. "Time, Eddie," he said. "Let's play ball!"

"Play ball! Play ball!" roared the stands. "Play ball!"

Duer glanced at the runners perched on the bases and then at the next hitter, the Raptors' big first baseman. It was a tough spot. Jack Castillo could hit the long ball.

Castillo did hit the long ball—one of the longest ever seen in Hedgetown! He met Kildane's fastball right on the nose, and the ball rocketed high over and beyond the left-field wall. It was a grand-slam blow, a homer in any park in the land, and the Raptors were way out in front with four runs across and no one out.

That did it! Duer barked, "Time!" and was out of the dugout like a shot, his face an angry red. He motioned to Curry and Kildane and waved the others away. "All right, Scissors, you're giving your own signs. Curry, you shake him off if you don't like them, but don't give any signs. This has gone far enough!"

Bill Malloy had the same opinion. He knew Eddie Duer had been right. Someone was giving the signs away, and if Chip Hilton could call the pitches, why couldn't the Raptors? He rose abruptly and started for the dugout, threading his way through the electrified Raptors fans. By the time he reached the dugout, Conover had walked, Roth had sacrificed the runner to second, and Kildane was pitching to Kinkaid.

"You're right," Malloy puffed, dropping heavily down on the bench beside Duer. "Chip called every shot. I thought you changed the signs."

"Did! Even put in an addition set too! But you saw what happened."

"Is Scissors right?"

"Mickey says he's never been better."

"What you doing about the signs now?"

"Kildane's giving his own. Maybe that will—"

Duer never finished that sentence. Kinkaid smacked a hard one, and Conover came tearing in from third.

Kinkaid had always been an automatic out for Kildane, for the whole Bears pitching staff as far as that was concerned. But he'd met this fastball on a full count with the meat of the bat, carrying it all the way to the fence in right center. Kinkaid slid safely into third just ahead of Klein's peg. That made it 5-0, with a man on third, one down, and Corey Berry at bat.

Kildane was desperate. He had never experienced anything like this! He decided to pitch to the Raptors as if he'd never faced them before. Scissors surprised Curry by using only his fastball. And he surprised Corey Berry too. Berry liked a fastball, letter high, and Kildane gave it to him right down the pipe for a called strike. He came right back with another and then another. Berry got a piece of the first one, but he missed the next one a country mile for the out.

Pitcher Skids Baker tipped his batting helmet to the crowd, and the thunder from the stands was deafening. But the fireball hurler couldn't handle his own stock in trade, the fastball. Kildane's smoker was jumping, and Baker went down swinging on three dazzling streaks of light that split the plate.

The Bears came hustling in, but they were worried. They couldn't understand what was happening. Damon Boyd grabbed Curry by the arm. "What's up with the signs?" he demanded.

"You keepin' 'em secret?" Squill barked. "What are we supposed to do? Guess what Kildane's gonna throw?"

"Ask Eddie," Curry said shortly. "It's his orders!"

Duer sprang up out of the dugout, nodding seriously as the players faced him. "That's right," he said evenly. "My orders! They're still getting the signs, so Scissors is flashing them to Curry, and the rest of you are on your own."

DUGOUT JINX

The news was received in dead silence. Their eyes registered dismay, and the surprise and shock were so great they forgot it was their turn at bat. They were roused into action only by the plate umpire's raucous, "Play ball!"

"Play ball!" rolled down from the stands as the Hedgetown fans exulted in the pennant surge of the Raptors, but the Bears seemed to have lost all desire to play ball. They were shocked, barely going through the motions. A player had to be up when he was playing a clutch game in a tight pennant race! Way up! But a player couldn't fight when his confidence in his own teammates was shattered.

Damon Boyd and Paul Hale exchanged long, bewildered glances, and Norman Klein and Stretch Johnson stiffly moved away from the bat rack. Klein knelt in the on-deck circle and leaned on his bat, but he didn't speak to Johnson in his usual cheery manner. He didn't yell, "Get on, Stretch. I'll bring you in!" No, Klein was looking down at the ground trying to figure it all out.

Stretch Johnson cast a quick glance at the dugout and then at Eddie Duer in the third-base coaching box. He slowly stepped up to the plate. Johnson's arms felt lifeless, drained of all their strength. He swung that way too—three times. When the inning ended, the fans cheered Skids Baker for his three straight strikeouts, and the Bears walked out to their positions a beaten team.

The less said about that game—if it could be called a game—the better. The Raptors beat up the Bears 9-0. Hedgetown was out in front in the pennant race with one game to go, sure of a tie in the final standings and, judging by the way the Bears were playing, unbeatable!

Yes, it looked bad for the Bears.

"What happened to Kildane?"

"You guys gonna show up tomorrow?"

"One down and one to go, and you guys are playin' for second place!"

"You kissed the pennant good-bye today! If Kildane couldn't do it, no one can!

"Didn't have it in the clutch, did ya? Ya bums!"

CHAPTER 17

A Great Comeback

BILL MALLOY had watched his team go to pieces that afternoon. He knew putting the pieces together again would take superhuman effort. The Bears had been a team until that fateful first inning. Following that disastrous start, Duer's abrupt announcement about the signs—that the team was on its own and Scissors Kildane was giving his own signs—had turned the team of talented youngsters into a collection of individuals playing sandlot baseball.

Sandlot baseball wasn't going to beat the Raptors the way they were going! That was why Malloy followed the players to the clubhouse and why Eddie Duer called them together after they had showered and dressed.

"Men," Malloy began, "this is the first time this year I've felt it was necessary to talk to you about your play on the field." He gestured toward Duer.

"Eddie is a great manager, has my full confidence, and I know he understands I'm taking this step only because I feel it's necessary."

A GREAT COMEBACK

The Bears shifted uneasily in their seats, wondering what was coming next. After a brief pause, Malloy continued. "I saw a great team fall apart this afternoon. I saw a bunch of players who had banded themselves together with tremendous fighting spirit suddenly lose all their poise and hustle. And I know why! Because they lost confidence in one another.

"You men forged to the top of the Midwestern League to the surprise of everyone except Eddie Duer and me. Eddie and I knew you had it! We know you still have it! You have what it takes to come back and win the pennant. Tomorrow's game is a must! It has to be won! But it isn't going to be won unless we can regain our team spirit. That's what we have to do tonight!

"I've asked Eddie to call a meeting for nine o'clock. I want every player there because we're going to decide on a set of signs to use tomorrow. Win, lose, or draw! Not only for the catcher and the pitcher but for the team— just as we've used them all year."

Chip listened with mixed emotions. Changing the signs wouldn't do any good as long as Corky Squill was giving them away. They could change the signs every pitch, and Squill could still give them away. Chip glanced at the fiery second baseman. Squill was completely lodged in his shell, looking straight ahead. Corky was a hard nut to crack, difficult to figure out.

Two hours later, Chip began packing his suitcase. He folded the Bears uniform carefully and spread it on the bed. Despite his protests, Eddie Duer had made him take it, had patted him on the shoulder and said, "We want you to have it, Chip. Just as a souvenir, even if you never wear it again."

He'd wear it all right, Chip was thinking. He'd be proud of it as long as he lived. Chip wished he could stay for the last game. That game was really going to be something to see! But he had to go home as he'd planned.

He smoothed out the uniform and walked over to the window. He was lonely, and a heaviness that wouldn't go away weighed on his chest. He could still feel the friendly handshakes of Scissors, Duer, Bill Malloy, and Mickey Curry when they'd said good-bye. They sure were a great bunch . . . didn't deserve to lose the pennant because of trickery or deceit . . .

Chip glanced at his watch. He still had an hour. He sat on the bed and tried to figure out what he ought to do about Corky Squill.

He knew Eddie, Scissors, and Mickey were at that moment planning a new set of signs. They wanted to have them ready before the team meeting. Chip didn't think Duer or Kildane or Curry would be able to do anything about the signs. There didn't seem to be much he could do about it either. Time was running out. Maybe he could have given Scissors a better lead.

Chip's thoughts swung to Valley Falls. This time tomorrow he'd be home. But, before he left Parkville, something had to be done about Corky Squill. Someone had to talk to Corky, and he was the only person to do it.

Gabby Breen wanted to talk to Corky Squill too. The scrappy infielder was very much in the Raptors manager's thoughts. Breen had been thrilled by the big win that put the Raptors in the lead, but he'd been worried for eight solid innings. Something had gone wrong, and the wily manager wanted to be sure it was straightened out before the final game. He watched the clock and fretted and fussed and paced the floor. Eventually he began to talk out loud, voicing his thoughts.

A GREAT COMEBACK

"Wonder what happened? Good thing we got those five runs in the first inning! Put them in a hole! Gotta be sure about tomorrow. Everything's gotta click. How about a team trailin' the whole season and then goin' out in front in the next to the last game? Bet Eddie Duer ain't feelin' so hot tonight! Hope he feels the same way tomorrow night. Why doesn't that little jerk call? Shootin' his mouth off somewhere, I s'pose!"

Corky Squill wasn't "shootin' his mouth off." He was listening—listening to Chip Hilton. Chip had found him in the lobby, waiting for the nine o'clock meeting. The lone wolf was nervous, and just when Chip thought he might have to face Squill right there in front of the others, the lonesome second baseman walked out the front door and headed down the street. Chip followed, catching up with him near the middle of the block.

"Could I talk with you for a minute, Corky?"

Squill turned around in startled surprise. "What's that?" he demanded harshly. "What did you say?"

"I said I'd like to talk to you about the signs," Chip said evenly.

Squill's eyes narrowed, and he moved a step closer to Chip, measuring the distance to the teenager's chin. "Signs?" he echoed, lowering his voice. "What signs?"

"The team signs," Chip said patiently. "The signs for the pitcher."

Corky's eyes glittered angrily. He clenched his fists and expanded his chest. "Look, Hilton," he grated, "I don't want to talk to you about anything! Period! Get lost, Jinx!"

"Would you rather I told Eddie Duer?"

"What do I care who you tell? I don't know what you're talkin' about."

"I'm talking about the way you give away the signs."

DUGOUT JINX

"*I* give away the signs," Squill growled, moving forward. "Why you—"

"Just a second, Corky," Chip said calmly. "You give away the signs for every pitch. I've been behind the plate the last two games, and I called every pitch—just by watching you. If I can call them by watching you, so can Gabby Breen!"

Squill was on the verge of slugging Chip. "What's that?" he asked, stopped by the mention of Gabby Breen. "You can call the signs by watching me?"

"That's right!"

Squill listened while Chip described every move Corky made in the field and explained its relation to the pitch. As Chip talked, he watched Corky warily, prepared for the worst. But the infielder's face was a blank; only his glittering eyes revealed his intense interest.

"Every time Curry signals for a fastball to a right-handed hitter, you move two or three steps to the left and back," said Chip, watching Squill closely. "All Breen has to do is see your move and pass the information to his hitter from the third-base coaching box. When a fastball is coming to a left-handed hitter, you take two or three steps to the right and back, don't you, Corky? And when Curry signals for a curve or slider—do you want me to go on, Corky?"

A bewildered Corky eyed Chip ominously. Standing with his hands on his hips, he coldly appraised the tall athlete.

"Pretty smart, aren't you?" he stated bitterly. "Did you say anything to anyone else about this?"

"No, not about your part in it. I told Scissors I could call the pitches and proved it, and I did the same with Mr. Malloy, but I didn't tell them how I could do it."

"And you didn't tell a single soul you were watchin' me?"

"No."

Squill's eyes drilled Chip through and through as he searched Chip's face. "Why not?" he asked suddenly and sharply. "Why didn't you?"

"Because I don't play ball that way. I couldn't! Well, I'm sorry we couldn't be friends, Corky, and I'm sorry about the signs."

"Just a minute," Squill said quickly. "How come you're tellin' me all this now?"

"Because I'm hoping you can do something about it before tomorrow's game."

"And you ain't gonna tell anyone else?"

Chip shook his head. "No, Corky," he said firmly. "I'm not going to tell anyone anything—ever. Now, I've got to go."

Chip hurried into the hotel, and Corky was still standing in the same spot when he emerged a few minutes later. Chip lifted his arm in a farewell wave, but Squill never moved. After Chip's taxi pulled away, Corky walked slowly down the street and around the corner to his usual phone booth and called Gabby Breen.

Breen was waiting and grabbed the receiver before the end of the first ring. "Hello, Corky. Sure glad you called. Was getting worried. . . . It wasn't your fault! The rest of them bums quit! All but Kildane. Well, tomorrow's another day. . . . Hope not! Say, Kearns said I was to contact Duer soon as it's over and what d'ya think? He wants me to talk trades with Eddie, and you're the man he wants! I told you it would work out, didn't I? . . . He said to go the limit! That means he's sold on you for his field captain. Now, look, Corky. Tomorrow's the big day for both of us. Put out for all you're worth. Kearns will be watchin' you the whole game, and he'll be imaginin' you in a Raptors uniform and playin' for Hedgetown next year. So make it good! OK?"

Corky Squill passed a fretful night, tossing, turning, and thinking. Sunday morning brought no relief. That was partly the reason he missed the bus and had to hurry out to the park in a taxi. His teammates were on the field when Squill reached the dressing room. He dressed quickly and ran out through the dugout to meet more trouble. Eddie Duer was standing there and gave Squill the bad news.

"You're late! That'll be fifty dollars out of your pocket, Corky," Duer said coolly, turning abruptly away.

"That's all right," Squill said softly. "Don't worry about it."

Minutes later the players and the fans scrambled to their feet and stood at attention while the strains of "The Star-Spangled Banner" filled the stadium. They listened silently at first, but the lift of the anthem got under their skins, and one by one they joined voices until it was a mighty chorus. On the last note a great shout went up, and the Raptors dashed onto the field. Corky Squill readied himself at the plate. The crucial game was on.

Chip had been glad to get away from the confusion and worry during the hectic days of the past week. He settled in his seat, but his mind refused to rest. It carried him right back to Hedgetown, and he was weary and downhearted until he drifted off to sleep.

They were all there, just as Chip had expected! Soapy Smith saw him first and jumped up and down as he waved. He was mouthing something, but Chip couldn't make out the words. It didn't matter. Moments later, Soapy, Biggie Cohen, Speed Morris, Red Schwartz, Petey Jackson, Taps Browning, and a dozen other friends were hugging him and slapping him on the back.

A GREAT COMEBACK

Chip was home! But his eyes searched everywhere until they found her—his mom waiting at the edge of the noisy group. He didn't realize how much he'd missed her! He lifted Mary Hilton in his arms, swinging her around in their old familiar way.

Seconds later, Chip's buddies were at him again, and with his arm around his mom, he let them pull him along to the street where Speed's Mustang and his mom's car were parked. Speed and Biggie hopped into the red fastback while Chip got behind the wheel of their car. The rest of the crew piled in wherever they could squeeze. There, all semblance of order ended. The back seats were a jumble of arms, legs, and bodies until the cars pulled into the driveway of 131 Beech Street.

The Hilton Athletic Club, friends all through high school, was together again! By two o'clock the missing members had all arrived and had joined Chip in the family room to listen to the game.

"—Kildane is one of the tallest pitchers in the minors, you know. There's the stretch—the pitch—it's in there for a called third strike, and that's all for the Raptors. Now here's Bud Lewis with a message for you. Bud—"

Biggie Cohen talked over the commercial. "Might have a couple of cracked ribs, but there isn't anything wrong with his arm," he said in admiration.

"That's his twelfth strikeout," Soapy announced. "Is he hot!"

"No one has reached first yet!"

"Twelve strikeouts in six innings! Wow! Let's see, at that rate he'll have eighteen."

"We can count!"

"And multiply!"

The babble of excited voices gave Chip his first chance to think. His pals had thrown questions at him every minute since he'd been home, and the game had been so exciting he hadn't even thought about the signs.

There wasn't anything wrong with the signs the Bears were using now! So far, Scissors had held the Raptors to one hit while the Bears had driven Baker to the showers and had scored nine times. Corky Squill had scored three of those runs and had played sensationally in the field. What if he'd been wrong about Corky?

Forty minutes later it was all over, and the Bears and the Raptors had finished the season even, each with 48 victories and 29 defeats.

"—So that winds it up, ladies and gentlemen. This is George Marsh signing off for Bud Lewis and the Benchley Company."

"Eleven to one!"

"What a game!"

"That means three out of five."

"With the first two games at Hedgetown and the second two at Parkville."

"What if they have to play the fifth game? Where will they play it?"

"Didn't ya hear the guy say the fifth game would be played at Hedgetown?"

"*Won't* be no fifth game! Won't even be four!" Soapy asserted. "Now that Kildane's back in form! He'll kill 'em. He'll kill 'em!"

Chip grinned. The Hilton A. C. had sure adopted the Bears. He wished he was in the Bears' locker room right then. It probably was a madhouse.

Chip was right. It was, indeed, a madhouse—an exuberant madhouse! The players were as spontaneous as little boys having a pillow fight at a sleepover. Paul Hale had torn Johnson's straw hat to shreds, and the big first baseman retaliated by chasing the feisty third baseman under the showers in full uniform. It was glorious fun, a great comeback.

Kildane tried to put through a call on the clubhouse phone but had to give up. The Bears weren't standing for any such nonsense. That was the reason he had to call Chip from the hotel two hours later.

"Did you hear the game, Chip? How'd you like it? Thought I'd call anyway. The playoff series starts Tuesday. Eddie said he was going to use Richards, but he might change his mind. I've got something important to tell you, but I can't do it now. Something about the signs. I'll give you the whole story after the playoff series. You'll be amazed!"

CHAPTER 18

Four for Four

WILLIAM MALLOY was a happy man. Hadn't his Bears won two straight playoff games from the Raptors, and weren't the Parkville fans storming the gates and standing in lines extending clear around Bears Stadium? To top it off, Eddie Duer had gotten by with Troy Richards in Tuesday's game and with Windy Mills in Wednesday's game. That is, for eight innings.

Duer had called Kildane out of the bullpen to put out the fire when Mills got into trouble in the eighth. With the Bears leading 4-2 and one gone, the Raptors had loaded the bases on a single and two walks. But, true to form, Kildane had taken personal care of that little emergency by striking out Marreno and Castillo and, in the bottom of the ninth, had set Conover, Roth, and Kinkaid down in order.

Malloy grinned at his manager and asked, "Is Scissors all right?"

"Right? Can't hold him! He even wanted to throw yesterday."

"Ribs bother him?"

"Says no, but you know him. Well, I'm going down-stairs and suit up."

"Relax, Eddie," Malloy protested. "It's only ten o'clock. You've got another hour. By the way, are you changing the signs again today?"

"No, we're going with the same set."

Malloy was puzzled. "I'll never understand that. I still think Hilton was guessing."

Eddie Duer said nothing, but before he could control them, little laugh wrinkles twitched at the corners of his mouth. Malloy's sharp glance caught them, and he gave Duer a long, suspicious look. "Are you holding out on me, Eddie?"

"Well, I wouldn't say I was holding out, boss."

"But you know something about the signs that I don't—is that it?"

Duer nodded. "Yes, boss, I do! But I'd rather not tell you about it until the series is over."

"That means this afternoon," Malloy said pointedly. "All right, but just as soon as the game is over, I want you to tell me."

"Right! And you'll get the shock of your life!"

Chip Hilton had enjoyed a series of shocks—all pleasant. He had been anxiously awaiting the game on Tuesday when every member of the Hilton A. C. packed the family room to listen to the game from Hedgetown. Chip had been thrilled by Corky Squill's great playing and by the Bears' 7-5 victory. But the 4-2 win on Wednesday had been the biggest surprise. No one would've believed the Bears could take the Raptors for two in a row in front of their hometown fans, but the Parkville team had done just that! Now, anything could happen.

Before Chip realized it, the game was underway. Kildane and Curry started for the Bears. For the Raptors, it was Baker and Berry. Just as expected, the game developed into one of those tension-tight pitchers' duels where the breaks could mean victory or defeat.

The Bears drew first blood in the third. Hale drew a free ride, Curry sacrificed him to second, and the hot-corner guardian slid safely into third on Kildane's fielder's choice. Then Corky drove in the run with a sharp single to right, and the Bears were out in front, 1-0.

That's the way it stood until the seventh when Kildane poured a third-strike screwball low and inside to Nick Marreno. The Raptors first baseman swung, and the ball spun off Curry's glove. Before Mickey could recover the twisting speed ball, Marreno was on second, with none away. Kildane then worked Jack Castillo to the one-and-two count. But on an inside waste pitch, Castillo fell away and the ball hit his bat for one of those freak infield dribblers no one can explain. The ball went twisting and spinning down the third-base line, and Castillo beat Hale's throw by an eyelash. That put Marreno on third, and Conover's sacrifice squeeze bunt scored Marreno and advanced Castillo to second.

Then Roth broke Chip's heart by connecting with an inside fastball, sending the ball streaking down the hot-corner chalk line all the way to the left-field fence. Jack Castillo scored to make it 2-1 in favor of the Raptors, and the tally held going into the last of the ninth.

There wasn't a sound in the room as Chip and his friends concentrated on the Bears' final time at bat. Soapy even stayed out of the refrigerator to listen and was strangely silent. Hale walked and Curry's attempted sacrifice resulted in a pop fly to Berry, who fired the ball to first just missing the double play. It was Kildane's turn to hit.

FOUR FOR FOUR

"Well, folks, is Duer really going to let Kildane hit? I really doubt it! Last of the ninth—behind two to one—a runner on first with one down. Oh, my! Duer is letting Kildane step into the batter's box. Can't understand this kind of baseball strategy. I don't want to second-guess Eddie Duer, but in my book this calls for a pinch hitter. That's why Ketch Kerrigan is on this team. I'm afraid Eddie may pay dearly for this decision."

Biggie was shaking his head. "This is bad," he said sourly. "Kildane can't hit."

"Quiet," Chip whispered. "He can bunt."

"—Kildane's not too good with the stick. The situation calls for a pinch hitter. Kildane will probably lay one down—I can't see this kind of strategy.

"Scissors is taking his time getting up there. He's a big man, you know, six-six. He's had none for three today. Bats from the third-base side of the plate.

"Baker sets—there's the stretch—here's the pitch—low and outside for ball one. They pitch 'em low and outside or high and inside to this big guy. The Raptors are playing in close."

Just then Petey Jackson came charging down the hall and elbowed his way into the family room. "What happened?" he exploded. "Who's win—"

"Be quiet!"

"—around the knees and caught the outside corner to even the count. One and one now, and Kildane steps out of the box. He's looking down the line at manager Eddie Duer in the third-base coaching box—this is an important pitch."

Chip's thoughts raced back to his last talk with the tall pitcher. Kildane had stressed the importance knowledge of the opposing hitters' weaknesses played in a pitcher's success. "They sure know mine," he had said wryly. "I haven't looked at a ball near the middle of the strike zone since I hit the league."

"—and it's low and outside. Two and one now, and Kildane's ahead of Baker. There's bad blood between these two.

"Baker stretches—lowers his hands—here's the pitch. It's high and inside, and it's too close. Kildane didn't move a muscle. He's got guts. He wants on. Listen to this crowd. Three and one now, and Berry is calling time and walking out to the mound. There goes Gabby Breen. He might pull Baker. The big pitcher's got himself in a hole now.

"Kildane's out of the batter's box. He's looking at Duer. Squill's in the on-deck circle. He's had three for three today. Folks, I can't understand Duer's strategy. He could put Kerrigan in to bat for Kildane even now. Lots of fans are yelling for Ketch right now, but Duer's ignoring them. I guess he's playing for the tie run.

"It's a cinch the Raptors aren't going to let that winning run get on, not with Squill on deck."

Chip couldn't understand any part of this game; he couldn't understand Corky Squill. What if he'd been wrong? It sure looked like it. Corky had hit three straight times and had scored the only run for the Bears.

"Kildane's back in the batter's box now. He isn't scared up there. The big man crowds the plate, and when he hinges those long arms and sticks his *elbows out over the plate—well, he's tough to throw to. Puts all the pressure on Baker. Skids might pass him—might hit him too and put the winning run on base.*

"Gabby Breen sure doesn't want Baker to pass Kildane, not with Mister Poison on deck. No, he'll pitch to Scissors. Here comes Breen. He's going to ride it out with Baker.

"Kildane could win his own game and the pennant on this next pitch—if he could park one over the fence. He's got the power, but every pitcher in the league knows his weakness for the high and the low pitches. The Raptors are playing deep now, playing for the force and the double play.

"Baker stretches—it's a tense moment; you can hear a pin drop here right now. Here comes the pitch. Kildane's taking it—it's in there, right across the middle of the plate. It's a called strike for the full count! Hear that crowd! This is real baseball drama, and it's the first time I ever saw a pitcher put one across the middle for the big guy."

Soapy couldn't stand the tension. He shuffled his feet and cleared his throat and managed a hoarse whisper. "Knock it out, Scissors, ple-e-ase."

"—and here it comes—it's a—"
"C-R-A-C-K!"

Chip heard the thunderous cheer almost as soon as he heard the crack of the bat, but that was all he could hear even though the announcer was shouting at the top of his voice. It seemed an eternity before he could hear the play-by-play.

"—right on the nose and beat it out! I'll never know how Bates made that stop. The ball was far to his right, but he dove for it and made a backhand stop and held Curry at second. Bates might have caught Curry on the play if he hadn't been lying on the ground, because Mickey had made the turn and barely beat the throw back to the bag.

"Breen's out on the field now. The winning run is on, and Breen doesn't like that. Time is out and the Raptors dugout is riding Corky Squill, and Squill's giving it right back to them.

"This is a tense moment, folks, and you can understand the bench jockeying I'm sure. The whole Raptors team and the fans and Gabby Breen and every player in the Raptors dugout will be on Squill now.

"Breen's starting back to the dugout. He's yelling at Squill through cupped hands again, and the Bears star is giving it right back. Here comes Eddie Duer. Duer's running toward Breen—looks like there's going to be trouble. They're nose to nose now! There they go! The players are running up—and here comes the umpiring crew. Both dugouts have completely emptied! They're swinging—Duer and Breen are flailing away at each other. The umpires have got them separated. The rhubarb is all over! Some fun! As usual, most of the action took place with their mouths!

"The umpires are taking charge now. Now wait a minute—hold everything. They've tossed Breen and Duer out. Yep. There they go, both of them.

"Bob Reiter is taking Duer's place in the third-base coaching box. Baker is ready to pitch. Squill is stepping into the box. Runners on first and second.

Mickey Curry's on second with the tying run, and Scissors Kildane is on first with the winning run. Corky Squill's at bat—one of the best infielders in the business, you know—been in a bad slump for the past few weeks, but he's sure out of it now. Came out of it just in time for the Sunday game when the Bears had to win. Squill's had three for three so far in this one, and he's up there now with a chance to win the game.

"Baker stretches. He's looking back at Curry on second. The Raptors will be playing for the double play. Curry's taking a short lead off second. Kildane is just a step away from first. Here's the pitch—it's outside.

"Baker stretches. He's looking back at Curry—seems nervous. It's a strike. Turner and Buster Lewis are throwing harder in the Raptors bullpen. One and one.

"Squill steps back out of the box, and Baker steps back off the hill. This is a tense moment. Corky's back in there now. Here comes the pitch. Squill swings—foul. Squill got a piece of it—it's back on the screen. One and two now. Baker's ahead of Squill now—won't give the little guy anything good."

Chip just couldn't understand it. But he knew one thing. He must have been wrong about Corky Squill. It was even possible he'd been wrong about the whole thing.

"—that evens the count now, and this suspense is almost unbearable. You can almost hear it crackle through this crowd.

"Baker stretches—lowers his arms—holds it there a second. Here's the pitch.

"C-R-A-C-K!"

DUGOUT JINX

The force of the cheering vibrated through the speakers as if the Hilton A. C. were right there in the ballpark. The clamor and the continuous crowd roar completely drowned out the announcer and every sound except the mad booming of thousands of voices into unintelligible reverberation.

Chip didn't hear the announcer, so he didn't know that Corky Squill had tripled against the right-field wall, that Curry had scored standing up, and that Scissors Kildane had slid almost from third base headlong with his long right arm stretched out through and beyond catcher Corey Berry to score the winning run and clinch the pennant for the Bears!

Chip knew the Bears had won; he knew it in his heart because it was right. And while the announcer shouted, Chip was out on that field chasing Scissors toward the dugout and joining the Bears in lifting the happy hurler to their shoulders. Yes, Chip was one of those who pounded Corky Squill on the back and pulled his cap down over his eyes and then helped hoist Eddie Duer up in the air! Chip saw the constant explosions of light as photographers and fans took the pictures of the new champions of the Midwestern League. And all the time he was thinking of the tragic mistake he'd made about Corky Squill.

As the noise thinned out, the radio announcer, yelling at the top of his voice directly into his mike, began to make his voice heard.

"—a madhouse, fans—absolutely a madhouse! These Parkville fans are down on the field now, and they've got Eddie Duer, Scissors Kildane, and Corky Squill up on top of the dugout, and they're throwing hats and programs, and shouting and yelling and cheering. And now they've got Bill Malloy, the owner of the Bears—"

Chip then realized that Soapy, Red, Biggie, Speed, and Taps were pounding and punching him, and he heard them for the first time.

"They did it, Chipper! They did it!"

"Let's celebrate! Food!"

"Let's call 'em!"

"Corky Squill! What a player!"

"What about Kildane!"

"Yeah, and that Eddie Duer!"

They acted as if Valley Falls had won that pennant, as if Eddie Duer, Scissors Kildane, and the Bears were local heroes. And, indeed, they were—to Chip Hilton and every member of the Hilton A. C.!

CHAPTER 19

Two Men and a Cat

THE PARKVILLE FANS wouldn't go home, and the stadium security didn't bother doing anything about it. Bill Meadows and his crew of groundskeepers were simply swept along like leaves before an October breeze when they tried to keep the crowd of excited spectators off the precious infield.

Under the grandstand and in the clubhouse the joyous crowd was packed so tight that the Bears couldn't even get to their lockers. They were surrounded by admiring fans who wanted to shake their hands. It took the Bears an hour to get themselves inside and keep the fans outside the locker room. By that time they were exhausted. They sat in front of their lockers and relaxed for the first time in days.

"That play-off bonus is gonna give me a long rest, and I need it!"

"I'm gonna spend forever on the Bighorn River fly-fishing. Those big trout are probably knocking on my cabin door right now!"

"What a crowd! I never saw anything like it!"

"Scissors, you old goat, I could kiss ya! I think I will!"

"How about that Corky? Four for four and that last one—Hey, where is Corky?"

"I haven't seen him since he hit that ball!"

"Maybe he's been locked out!"

"The door isn't locked now."

"How about Eddie? Anyone seen Eddie?"

"Haven't seen him since he was ejected!"

"There's something screwy goin' on here. Where's Mr. Malloy? We win the pennant and the big wheels disappear?"

"You suppose Corky's in trouble?"

"No, he's probably signing autographs and posing for photos. Would someone answer that crazy phone!"

They had all heard the persistent ringing but had ignored it. Finally, Bob Reiter picked it up.

"Hello, clubhouse. . . . Yeah, Eddie? . . . Sure! Everyone but Corky. . . . Oh, he is! Well, that's good. We were gettin' worried. . . . Yes, yes, I'm listening. . . . OK, I've got it. Party at Sullivan's, Friday night, and there's a meeting at the hotel tomorrow afternoon. . . . Sure, I'll tell them! See you in the morning!"

The players waited expectantly. Reiter's one-way conversation had peaked their curiosity.

"What's up?" Curry demanded.

Reiter grinned. "Just the usual—everything and anything," he drawled. "Malloy and Duer are tied up, but they said they knew all along you could do it, and they'll tell you personally tomorrow. Corky's with them in the office, and there's a mandatory meeting at four o'clock tomorrow at the park. The party's at Sullivan's at eight o'clock tomorrow night. And, Scissors—they want to see you right away."

"That all?" Hale queried innocently.

"Something's going on," Klein said flatly. "You know what it is?"

"I just work here, my winning friend," Reiter said pointedly. "Why don't you ask them yourself? There's the phone."

They turned on Kildane, then, besieging him with questions, but he was as much in the dark as Reiter.

Curry grunted. "Why worry? We'll find out all about it tomorrow."

"Probably be in the papers!" Johnson quipped. "I'm going to go get the biggest steak in town! See ya, Scissors. I'll wait for you at the hotel."

Johnson waited and so did about every other person in Parkville that evening. The Park Hotel was surrounded outside and jammed inside with fans who wanted to celebrate with the Bears—especially with Scissors Kildane and Corky Squill. But the two never showed up and didn't turn up until the next night.

Eddie Duer would say only that they had gone on a trip related to the banquet. The unusual duo showed up at Sullivan's Friday night—and they were accompanied by Chip Hilton!

Chip had hoped Scissors would call him right after Thursday's game, but the call never came. He was disappointed, but that was nothing compared to the shock he received early Friday morning. Chip and his mom had just finished breakfast when the doorbell rang. In fact, the bell never stopped.

"Cut it out, Soapy!" Chip shouted as he walked toward the door. "You'll wear that bell out." The ringing continued until Chip opened the door. There stood Scissors Kildane and Corky Squill holding a meowing Hoops under one arm! Chip could scarcely believe his eyes.

"Scissors? Corky?"

"That's us! Want a cat?" the duo couldn't stop laughing.

"What—what are you doing here?"

"We've come to get you! If you'll let the three of us in!" Kildane laughed, shoving Chip into the hallway. "Come on, get your banquet threads. You're goin' to Parkville with us, and we're leaving in ten minutes. It's a long drive."

"Parkville? Why?"

"Parkville?" Mary Hilton echoed. "What for?"

"That's right," Kildane said. "You're Chip's mom, aren't you? Anyone would know that! This is Corky Squill, Mrs. Hilton, and I'm Scissors Kildane. We talked on the phone once. Excuse us for being so abrupt, but Mr. Malloy, that's our boss, sent us here to get Chip and bring him back alive for the pennant banquet."

"But—"

"No buts and no ifs! We're taking Chip back with us. We'll take you, too, if you'll go! Those are Bill Malloy's orders."

"And orders is orders," Squill added. "Especially Mr. Malloy's!"

"But I can't," Chip protested. "I've got to leave Sunday for State."

"We'll get you back here early Sunday morning."

"But why? Why does Mr. Malloy want to see me?"

"What do you mean Malloy?" Kildane blustered. "How about the rest of us? We all want you to come. Don't we, Corky?"

Squill was emphatic. "We sure do! Especially me!"

Chip was completely confused by the friendly spirit between Scissors and Corky. Something had happened, and he was completely baffled.

Again he was chilled by the thought he'd misjudged Corky Squill. He was doubly bewildered by Corky's friendliness. What could have happened? And how did Corky get a black eye?

"*Well*, let's go," Kildane growled good-naturedly. "It's a long drive."

"Is it all right with you, Mrs. Hilton?" Squill asked.

"Sounds as if you two wouldn't take no for an answer anyway," Mary Hilton laughed. "If Chip wants to go—"

"All right, then," Kildane said happily, slapping Chip on the shoulder. "Let's go, we're burning daylight!"

They made it—a little tired and a little grimy, but on time. Chip was embraced by the happy ballplayers who were on top of the world. After dessert had been served, team owner Bill Malloy took charge of the program. "Men," the popular club owner began, "this dinner is no accident. Eddie and I planned it a long time ago as well as several other surprises we hope you're going to enjoy.

"At first we thought we'd make it big, invite the public. But we changed our minds toward the end of the race, and I think you'll enjoy this family gathering just as much.

"Now, for my personal surprises. I have some checks here. The pennant bonus checks, your salary checks, and a special club bonus check for each of you. I think you'll like the figures."

Bill Malloy got the answer right then in a tremendous round of applause. You could tell Bill Malloy appreciated the response, but he held up his hands for silence.

"Now for the next club surprise. Eddie Duer cooked this one up, so he gets the credit. Of course Eddie was kind enough to arrange things so I could pick up the tab."

A burst of laughter greeted that statement. Everyone in the room knew how well Eddie Duer could work money out of Bill Malloy.

"I'll assure you it didn't require much urging. Give me a hand here, Eddie, Bob."

Malloy picked up a small box and opened it. Everyone could see it was a ring with a diamond set in the middle of the baseball. It was a championship diamond ring! The rafters rang with applause again. Each player was presented his ring: Corky Squill, Damon Boyd, Bill Dawson, Stretch Johnson, Norm Klein, Ted Smith, Pauly Hale, Mickey Curry, and Scissors Kildane. Malloy called the batting order first, with Scissors Kildane in the ninth spot, and then he called the rest of the players and coaches. Finally, he called Eddie Duer.

The teammates nearly lifted the roof, then, giving the likable manager an ovation that brought tears to his eyes. He stood there unashamed, proud, and happy, until Malloy finally quieted the assembly and continued.

"That ends my part of the program. Eddie. You're on. Take over."

Eddie Duer needed time right then, and the roar of appreciation the players accorded Malloy served the purpose. Duer's voice was shaky, and the words came slow and hard at first.

"Thanks for everything. I've already expressed my thanks to Mr. Malloy."

"It was the checks!" Malloy said dryly.

That brought a tremendous laugh, and Duer was himself again when it quieted. He looked around and finally located the person he wanted.

"Now, I want to introduce Corky Squill. Corky has something to say, and he asked me if he might get it off his chest tonight. I know what he's going to talk about, and I'm sure you will remember it a long time. I guess I don't have to tell you that Corky Squill is, in my opinion, the best second baseman in the game."

Again the room rang with applause and cheers. If there was surprise in the hearts of some of those present, it wasn't evident in the tribute Squill received. Corky was embarrassed but determined, the same leadoff fighter who had played so brilliantly in the clutch games. Characteristically, he plunged right in.

"Thanks, Mr. Duer. I want to talk about the signs. All of you wondered what it was all about when the Raptors began to get our signs. Well, I'm the guy that gave them away."

In the dead silence that followed Corky's statement, Chip held his breath.

"Yes, I tipped our signs to the Raptors. Not intentionally, but because I was a bozo. Because I allowed myself to be bitter and jealous and small and the tool of an unscrupulous man.

"Yes, Gabby Breen manipulated me like a puppet on a string. He played on my ego and fed my jealousy and then used me unconsciously to betray my team.

"It's a long story, and I won't bore you with the details, but Gabby Breen started me in baseball, coached me, and was my first manager. He got to know me so well that he realized that I was giving the signs away by my motions and how I shifted position in the field. So Breen changed my style; he made me stand absolutely still after I got the signs, but he never told me why. He didn't tell me anything but a pack of lies then—and later.

"I had my little temper tantrums and got to whinin' because Eddie slapped a couple of fines on me. Then Gabby happened along and egged me on. That was before he knew he was goin' to manage the Raptors, but it's no excuse. I shouldn't have fraternized with him because he was a member of another organization.

"When Gabby saw he was goin' to get the managin' job, he really went to work on me and fed me a lot of lies about bein' the captain of the Raptors next year and gettin' a big increase in salary and everything. Then he gave me a line about Hunter Kearns likin' his second basemen to be hustlers, and he got me to change my style in the field right back to my old way of playin'.

"You know why, now. I fell for it. It was like takin' candy from a baby. Gabby said Kearns liked hustlin', jumpin'-jack, holler guys at second and as the team captain. You can see how stupid I was—and am.

"I have another ring Mr. Malloy gave me. He said I could have the honor of presentin' it to the guy who got wise to Breen's trickery and to my stupidity. I asked for the privilege of presenting it because I want to use the opportunity to apologize to him for a lot of ridin'.

"He made it possible for us to win the pennant. This guy told me what I was doin', how I was givin' the signs away, and I promptly told Eddie. We never let on to anyone else, but I just crossed up Mr. Gabby Breen by usin' my same old motions and actions—but for the wrong pitches.

"Gabby didn't get wise until the final game, and that's why I'm wearin' this little shiner. But that's another story. Right now I want to give this championship ring to the best teammate anybody ever had!

"I'm referrin' to Chip Hilton!"

Now Chip could see the whole picture. He never knew how he got up to that table or what he said, but he ended up wearing a championship baseball ring. The rest of that evening he shared a table with two of the finest friends he would ever have—Scissors Kildane and Corky Squill!

CHAPTER 20

A Token of Friendship

CHIP HILTON was the only quiet person in Speed Morris's red Mustang as they headed to the Sugar Bowl. Speed, Biggie, Red, and Soapy were firing questions at him from every direction. They wanted to talk about Scissors Kildane, Eddie Duer, Bill Malloy, Stretch Johnson, and Corky Squill.

The nearness of his friends and the pleasure they derived from hearing all about the banquet caused a surge of thankfulness to well up in Chip's heart. It was great to have friends like these, guys you'd grown up with and teamed up with on the football field, on the diamond, and on the court. It was great to make new friends too. His thoughts went speeding back to those last few minutes in Parkville when Kildane had left him alone with Corky, and Chip had come to know the real Corky Squill. Even now, Chip could hear the words the second baseman had spoken, and he could hear them just as if Corky was saying them all over again.

"You see, Chip, it's easy for some guys to fall under the influence of men like Gabby Breen. Lots of kids don't have good homes, fathers and mothers to guide them and help them with their problems. Not everybody has a chance to play on a school team and get good coachin' and the advice of a good man.

"I went to school only as long as I had to and then I quit. I always wanted to be a ballplayer, and Gabby Breen was the only person who ever paid any attention to me at all. Everyone else brushed me off and told me I'd seen too many movies."

Squill had grinned, then he continued. "I guess they were right. I always took in every sports movie I could, and whenever a baseball game was on, I was there. Then, one day, I was playin' in a sandlot game and, after the game, one of the guys said a big-league scout was in the stands and wanted to see me.

"I thought the guy was kiddin', but he wasn't. Breen *did* want to see me, and he took my name and address, but then I didn't hear any more from him, and I figured he'd forgotten me.

"But the next spring I got a letter to report to a little town in Ohio, and I took my glove and spikes and hitch-hiked there and tried out with about a hundred other kids. That night, Breen signed me to a contract.

"I was the happiest bozo in the world from that minute on, and Gabby Breen was the number one guy in my life.

"Then he got me in the Tri-State League and then Wilkton and then Parkville—and . . . well, I guess I'd a jumped off the bridge if Gabby had said to. Right after you showed up for the All-Star game, Gabby asked me to contact you, and I did. I figured I owed him any favor he asked. It didn't seem like a very big one at the time, especially when he said I could make three thousand dollars if you signed up with him. I'm sure glad you didn't!"

Squill had paused, then, and Chip could see the bitterness in Corky's eyes. After a moment he had continued, choosing his words carefully.

"Gabby kept leadin' me on and promisin' me I'd captain the Raptors and get a big increase in salary and all that stuff. That's why I went back to hustlin' the way I used to when I first started out. Only it wasn't hustlin', it was nervousness, mostly."

A little smile had played about the corners of Corky's mouth, and he had chuckled wryly. "I fell for it. Of course I didn't know what Gabby had in mind and—well, you know the rest. Gabby knew I gave the signs away with my motions and shiftin' around, and he figured he could call every pitch. He figured right too! I realize it now, but I never gave it a thought until you talked to me that night. I was pretty mad at the time, Chip.

"But after I thought it through, I knew you were right, and I realized how close I had come to lettin' down the team and playin' right into Breen's hands. Anyway, I crossed him up in the next game, and after we won the play-off I—but I'm gettin' ahead of my story.

"That Saturday night was the longest in my life. I thought about you and Breen and the team and the signs and how close I had come to losin' the pennant for all the guys and the people of Parkville and how close I had come to ruinin' my whole career. And then on Sunday mornin'—Chip, I hadn't been to church for years—but I went that Sunday. That's why I missed the bus to the park and the reason Duer slapped another fine on me. But it was worth it. It gave me the courage to go to Duer and tell him there would be no more sign stealin'. At the banquet it gave me the courage to stand up in front of the guys and tell them just what had happened. They're a pretty good bunch of guys, Chip.

"Oh, yes. I don't know whether anyone told you what happened after the championship game. Anyway, Breen found me in the crowd and socked me in the eye. That was bad news for him, because security grabbed him and rushed him up to Mr. Malloy's office. They sent for Mr. Kearns, and I told them the whole story. I guess you saw that Breen had resigned, only that wasn't exactly right. Mr. Kearns fired him right there in Mr. Malloy's office. He's out of baseball for good.

"Chip, I don't know how I can thank you for bein' such a good friend and havin' enough courage to come to me that night and tell me exactly what was goin' on. I wish I knew—"

Corky had stopped then, and Chip knew that the star second baseman's emotions had caught up with him. But Chip hadn't been prepared for Corky's next move. In fact, he hardly knew what had happened until later. Even now he could still hear the tremor in Corky's voice and feel the awkward handclasp.

"And . . . er . . . Chip, I wish you'd do me a favor. I wish you'd trade rings with me. I know our names are inscribed in them, but just wearin' your ring and lookin' at it once in a while will make me remember how close I came to makin' a terrible mistake. Maybe it'll keep me out of a lot of trouble sometime. That is, if you won't mind havin' *mine*."

Corky's voice had trailed off, but it hadn't mattered. Chip had slipped Corky's ring on his finger and had grasped the husky infielder's hand in a gesture of friendship and understanding. The clasped hands erased completely and forever all the ill feeling and rancor that once had burned in their hearts.

How easy it is to misjudge a person—and how easy to fall for a seemingly obvious fact. He could have ruined Corky Squill's reputation for life just because he'd believed the worst. Chip breathed a sigh of gratitude. He was sure glad he'd kept the details of his discovery to himself.

Now, as Chip absentmindedly turned the ring on his finger, he relived to the fullest one of those never-to-be-forgotten moments that comes to a person when someone who's been regarded as an enemy suddenly proves to be a friend and does something really big—acknowledges a mistake and is gracious enough to offer his most precious possession as a token of his friendship.

Suddenly Soapy's laughing voice cut through Chip's thoughts and brought him back to the present. Tonight Chip and his mom would drive to the university. Soon he'd be at State's football camp, and he'd be with the Rock again and making new friends and starting out on his quest for a college education.

"How about that!" Soapy shouted. "Mr. Malloy said he was gonna bring the whole team up to our first freshman game. You think he will?"

Chip grinned in the dark. He wasn't too sure William Malloy wouldn't do just that.

• • •

COACH CLAIR BEE'S *Freshman Quarterback* is literally packed with football, college life, campus intrigue, freshman pranks, and the spirit and traditions of a great university. Every reader who followed Chip Hilton's career at Valley Falls will be happy to find Chip, Soapy, Biggie, Speed, and Red carrying on in the same spirited manner at State University.

Afterword

MY GRANDFATHER, Clair Bee, introduced me to the Chip Hilton series when I was five years old. Today, Chip Hilton has returned, and I now have the privilege of contributing an afterword to the series that Poppop and I read together almost twenty years ago. I am tremendously proud of my parents' work and deeply appreciate the opportunity to join them in welcoming back Chip Hilton!

Clair Bee is most well known for his contributions to the game of basketball as an innovative coach with an unmatched winning percentage. If my grandfather were here today, however, he would tell you that success is not measured in mere wins and losses, but in how much of yourself you give to the game, to your profession, to your family, and to your community. As a father, grandfather, author, and coach, Clair Bee recognized that success in life would forever outweigh success in athletic competition. For some, winning at any cost is like a fever. It burns but never breaks. Winning requires much more than desire alone. My grandfather succeeded because he tempered his desire to win with a keen sense of right and wrong, a love of sport, and respect for those against whom he competed and usually defeated.

Chip Hilton personifies the combination of success in life and sport that catapulted my grandfather to the highest level of achievement in athletics. My grandfather's trophies, plaques, and awards have adorned the walls of our home for as long as I can remember. Of all his achievements, though, none shine so brightly as the Chip Hilton series. Contribution to sport is fleeting. Contribution to life, everlasting. My grandfather would be very pleased to know that through his contribution, the Chip Hilton series, he continues to give today even after he is gone.

I recently watched the film *Mr. Smith Goes to Washington* and was immediately reminded of the Chip Hilton series. Mr. Smith depicts a time when simple men with small-town values could arrive on the steps of the U.S. Capitol and, with a dose of honesty and integrity, right all of our nation's wrongs. To most, the movie simply depicts an era gone by. To others, however, Mr. Smith lends an inspirational vision of what America can once again become.

In many ways the Chip Hilton series not only depicts life as it used to be, but life as it should be. How close we come to that ideal depends upon how much we, as individuals, are willing to give as members of a larger community. The task of contribution is not simple, but we are fortunate to have many outstanding torchbearers. Coach Bob Knight and United States Senator Dan Coats stand out in my mind as two men who exemplify the principles of virtue and self-sacrifice practiced by my grandfather

AFTERWORD

and depicted in the Chip Hilton series. Coach Knight and Senator Coats have excelled in very different careers but share a common goal of personal excellence with a commitment to enrich the lives of those around them. We have a responsibility to continue their efforts. The path to success is never easy, but if Chip Hilton and Valley Falls are any indication of our potential as individuals and as a community, then the journey is certainly worthwhile.

MICHAEL CLAIR FARLEY

More Great Releases From The

by Coach Clair Bee

The sports-loving boy, born out of the imagination of Clair Bee, is back! Clair Bee first began writing the Chip Hilton series in 1948. During the next twenty years, over two million copies of the series were sold. Written in the tradition of the *Hardy Boys* mysteries, each book in this 23-volume series is a positive-themed tale of human relationships, good sportsmanship, and positive influences—things especially crucial to young boys. Through these larger-than-life fictional characters, countless young people have been exposed to stories that helped shape their lives.

WELCOME BACK, CHIP HILTON!

Vol. 1 - Touchdown Pass
0-8054-1686-2

Start collecting your complete Chip Hilton series today!

Available at fine bookstores everywhere.